Edward Bellamy, Richard Michaelis

Looking Forward

An answer to Looking Backward

Edward Bellamy, Richard Michaelis

Looking Forward
An answer to Looking Backward

ISBN/EAN: 9783337373047

Printed in Europe, USA, Canada, Australia, Japan

Cover: Foto ©Andreas Hilbeck / pixelio.de

More available books at **www.hansebooks.com**

Looking Forward

BY

RICHARD MICHAELIS,

Editor Chicago "Freie Presse."

~~~~~~~~~~

AN ANSWER TO

LOOKING BACKWARD

BY

EDWARD BELLAMY.

PREFACE.

EVERY seeker after truth and reform is entitled to recognition, even if his ways and methods are not ours. Mr. Edward Bellamy's book: "Looking Backward", is an effort to improve the lot of mankind and therefore commendable, but his reform proposition, stripped of its fine coloring, is nothing but communism, a state of society, which has proved a failure whenever established without a religious basis and which without such basis is en vogue today only among some barbarous and cannibal tribes.

Chicago has for the last fourteen years been the centre of the communistic and anarchistic agitation in the United States, and in defending the fundamental principles of American institutions against these theories, that were imported from the overcrowded industrial centres of Europe, I became quite familiar with them as well as with the notions and peculiarities of social reformers, who imagine themselves in possession of an infallible receipt to perfect not only all human institutions but also human nature.

Of course Mr. Bellamy holds more moderate views than those Spies and Parsons proclaimed, but he has this much in common with the Anarchists and Communists of Chicago: he has become incapable of passing a fair judgement upon our present institutions, conditions and men ; he overlooks all difficulties in the introduction of his proposed changes, he really believes his socialistic air-castles must spring into existence very soon and without obstruction, and he populates his fairy palaces with angelic human beings, who would never by any possibility do anything wrong. The surmise, that men and women in a communistic state, would put off all selfishness, envy, hate, jealousy, wrangling and desire to rule is just as reasonable as the supposition, that a man can sleep one hundred and thirteen years and rise thereafter as young and fresh as he went to bed.

What queer methods reformers sometimes advocate! John Most would in the name of equal rights to all, first kill all men who are not in absolute sympathy with his opinions, then abolish all laws and all officers, and then let nature take its course.—Mr. Bellamy on the other hand would, also in the name of equal rights, deprive all the clever and industrious workers of a large or the largest part of the products of their labor for the benefit of their awkward, stupid or lazy comrades! And this would be what Mr. Bellamy is pleased to style justice and equality!

And for the purpose of reaching this state of mock-equality, Mr. Bellamy would as a matter of course have to *sacrifice competition,* the gigantic power that elevated us all and Mr. Bellamy with us to the present state of evolution! It is true that competition has been and is now abused, but every institution is subject to abuse and the misuse of a thing does not demonstrate that the thing in itself is wrong. Nobody can deny that competition during the centuries of Christian civilization has developed the brains and muscles of the human race and that the continuous best efforts of humanity, stimulated by competition during these many centuries, have lifted our race to a standard where the mode of living of common laborers is more comfortable and desirable than the everyday existence of the Kings of which Homer sings.

Every generation has to battle with certain problems, and it is the lot of ours to overcome the difficulties between capital and labor, that have been increased by the change in the methods of production since the discovery of steam power.

We have to find ways and means not to avoid productive *work* (—spoken of by Mr. Bellamy as

an *evil*—), but to cure the brain cancer of our days:
the permanent uncertainty of subsistance and the
fear of poverty. And we accomplish this by co-
operation and by mutual insurance companies, without retrograding to communism, that most barbarous
state of society.

The imperfect nature of man characterizes, as a
matter of course, all human institutions and it is the
easiest thing in the world, by *"looking backward"*, to
find fault with living men as well as with the present
state of affairs and to build air castles inhabited by
angels only.

I will now *look forward!* By demonstrating what
would be the logical conclusion of Mr. Bellamy's
story, if fairly continued, I purpose to show that he
first tries to establish absolute equality and then,
despairing of success, advocates an inequality in
many respects more oppressive than the present state
of things. I intend to demonstrate, that under the
regime, proposed by Mr. Bellamy, favoritism and
corruption would be very potent factors in public
life. I expect to set forth that personal liberty would
fare so badly in Mr. Bellamy's United States, that
the proud and independent American people would
never tolerate such a system, and to prove beyond a
reasonable doubt, that the people would be much

poorer in Mr. Bellamy's condition of affairs, than at the present time.

I do not deny that our society stands in need of many desirable reforms; but I am not prepared to follow blindly Mr. Bellamy, John Most, or anybody else, who pretends that he is ready to deliver humanity from all evils on short notice, and I do not intend to jump head over heels into the dark.

If Mr. Bellamy and his followers are quite sure that they can establish the millennium, *let them try it,* like the communists of the Amana Society who have started a community in the state of Iowa on a religious basis. There are many thousands of acres of good government lands left, where Mr. Bellamy and his friends may settle and show the world what they can do! But they should not ask the people of the United States to break up their present form of government and state of society, before they have given their theories a trial and proved that their calculations are correct.

RICHARD MICHAELIS.

CHICAGO, April 1890.

LOOKING FORWARD.

CHAPTER I.

For the purpose of introducing myself to those readers of this book, who are not familiar with the contents of "Looking Backward", edited by Mr. Edward Bellamy, I will recapitulate the remarkable events of my life up to the end of that extraordinary narrative.

Born in Boston on the 26th day of December 1857, I was baptized Julian West, was educated in the schools and colleges of my city, but, being in possession of a handsome fortune, did not devote myself to any particular profession or trade. I became engaged to Miss Edith Bartlett, a young lady of great beauty, and it was our intention to marry as soon as my new house should be ready for occupation. The completion of the building was frequently delayed by strikes of masons and carpenters, and I occupied still the old fashioned house, where my family had lived for three generations.

Suffering from insomnia, I had prepared in the basement and under the foundations of the old building, a large vault, where the noises of a great city would not disturb me. This vault was absolutely fire-proof, and fresh air was assured by means of a small pipe running up to the roof of the house.

To obtain sleep I was frequently forced to avail myself of the services of a mesmerist, and it happened that on the 30th day of May 1887, after two sleepless nights, I sent my colored servant Sawyer to a Dr. Pillsbury, whom I was in the habit of employing. The doctor was about to leave the city to establish himself in New Orleans, and this was therefore the last time he would be able to treat me. I instructed Sawyer to rouse me at nine o'clock the next morning, and under the manipulations of the mesmerist I soon fell into a deep slumber.

When I opened my eyes again I found that I had slept 113 years, 3 months, and 11 days.

I discovered that the old house had been destroyed by fire and that Sawyer had perished in the flames. Dr. Pillsbury had left Boston, the existence of the vault where I slept was unknown to my friends, the house had not been rebuilt and so I remained in a mesmerized condition for over a hundred years, until a Dr. Leete, the occupant of a house which was being erected on a part of the old lot, commenced to build a laboratory and unearthed my vault in the year 2000.

I learned that Edith Bartlett, after mourning my loss fourteen years, had married, that Dr. Leete's wife was Edith Bartlett's granddaughter, and that his daughter Edith was therefore the great-granddaugher of the young lady who had been my promised bride 113 years before.

The vigor of my manhood of thirty years overcame the shock of these discoveries. I soon felt myself at home in Dr. Leete's house, the more so, because young Edith soon occupied the place in my heart once filled by Edith Bartlett, and it was not long before Edith Leete, a somewhat romantic, compassionate girl, consented with grace to become the successor of her great-grandmother; to be my bride.

But the turn of my own fate is even less remarkable, than the change that has taken place in the social order of things. Dr. Leete explained to me the new organization of society.

Individual enterprises have ended. The nation creates everything that individuals and corporations were producing at the end of the nineteenth century. Every able bodied man, every healthy woman belongs to the "industrial army". They enter the force at the age of 21 and are released at 45. Only in rare cases of necessity are men over 45 years of age summoned to work.

Money is abolished, but all inhabitants of the United States receive an equal share of the results of the work of the industrial army in the form of a credit card, a piece of paste board on which dollars and cents are marked. There is one store in each ward where people can select such goods as they may desire. The value of the goods, one purchases, is pricked out of his credit card and his account is charged in the Government books with the amount of goods so purchased.

The meals are furnished by large cooking houses. Washing and repairing are done in large laundries. One may take his meals home or eat them at the cooking house. The bill of fare is very elaborate and one may have even a special dining room. The amount to be paid for the meals differs of course according to the bill of fare ordered and to the place where the meal is taken.

Each family occupies a separate house; the furniture being the property of the tenant. The rent, which depends on the size of the house, is also pricked out of the credit card.

All inhabitants of the United States are obliged to attend school until they have reached the age of 21. Then they become members of the industrial army. During the first three years of their services they are called recruits or apprentices and have to do the common labor under the absolute command of the officers or overseers. A *record* is kept, in which are entered the ability and behavior of each recruit.

After the first three years of service, each recruit may select a profession or a trade. As far as possible the volunteers are placed in the trades they prefer. Recruits with the best records are given the first choice. Some of them have to take a second or third choice, and some are obliged to accept positions assigned to them by their superiors.

All members of the army are, according to their ability and behavior, divided into three grades, and apprentices with a first-class record may, after their three years service, enter at once the first grades of the different trades selected by them.

The general of the guild appoints all the officers of his trade. The lieutenants must be taken from the members of the first grades. The captains are chosen by the general from the lieutenants, the colonels from the captains. The general of the guild himself is elected by the former members of the trade, that is, those who have passed the age of forty-five. The ex-members of all the guilds also elect the chiefs of the ten great departments or groups of allied trades. The chiefs are taken from the generals of the guilds. And the former guild members also elect the President of the United States, who is taken from the ranks of the retired chiefs of the ten great departments. The President, the ten chiefs of the great departments and the generals of all the guilds live in Washington.

The members of the industrial army have not the right to vote for any of the officers by whom they are governed. They have no representation during their 24 years of service; but if they have a complaint against one of their superiors, they may bring their case before a judge whose decision is final.

The judges are appointed by the President from the ranks of the retired members of the guild for the term of five years.

Courts, lawyers, jails, sheriffs, tax-assessors, collectors and many other officers have been abolished. Criminals are treated in hospitals as persons mentally ill.

The National Government regulates the production. When it sees that certain trades attract a very large number of volunteers, while other trades fall short, the administration increases the working time of the preferred trades and shortens the working hours of those needing more volunteers.

The women have their own officers, generals, judges, and form an auxiliary army of industry. They receive the same credit cards as the men. Since the cooking and washing and repairing of household goods are done outside, the women of the twentieth century have more time for productive labor than had the women of a hundred years ago.

Recruits who have passed three years service, during which they are assignable to any work at the discretion of their superiors, may enter schools of technology, medicine, art, etc.; but if they cannot keep pace with the classes, they must withdraw. Physicians, who do not find sufficient employment, are assigned to work of another character.

If people desire the publication of a newspaper, they must club together and give up enough of their credit cards to compensate the nation for the loss of the work of the persons editing and printing the paper.

If one desires to publish a book, he can write it in his hours of leisure and can have it printed by giving up a part of his credit card. For the copies sold he receives again a new credit.

Preachers are in a similar way employed by persons who desire to hear their sermons

Cripples or other people unable to do full work or any work at all, receive their full credit cards, because the fact, that they are human beings, entitles them to their full share of all good things produced on earth.

The state governments within the United States have been abolished as useless.

All other civilized nations have organized themselves on a similar basis and are exchanging goods with each other. The yearly balances are settled with national staple articles.

The new order of things enables people to live without cares, and one of the consequences is the fact, that most of the men and women of an average constitution live from eighty-five to ninety years.—

Such was the description of the new order of things given me by Dr. Leete in a number of conversations. The doctor is very enthusiastic over the organization of society of the twentieth century and does not hesitate to call it the millennium.

The fear and uncertainty which I entertained in regard to my employment were set at rest by Dr. Leete, who said, that I could, if I wished, have the position of professor of the history of the nineteenth century in the Shawmut College of Boston. I have accepted the offer and shall enter upon my duties next Monday.

CHAPTER II.

WHEN I first entered the large hall of Shawmut College, where I was to deliver my lectures, I noticed near the door of the room a gentleman of about forty years of age. He was too old to be one of the students and as I had not seen him when Dr. Leete introduced me to the professors of the institution, I was somewhat curious to know in what capacity he honored my debut.

The cordial reception I had met at the hands of the professors, the fact that every seat of the large hall was occupied, acted as a stimulus and when Dr. White, the president of Shawmut College had introduced me with a few complimentary remarks as a living witness of the nineteenth century, I began my first lecture in the best of spirits.

My speech contained naturally many of the points that Dr. Leete had most dwelt upon, when, in his conversations with me, he had compared the organization of society of the nineteenth and that of the twentieth centuries.

I said in substance, that my hearers must not expect a synopsis of the civilization of the two centuries or a panegyric of the present state of affairs. I would point out but a few conditions, regulations and institutions that could serve as criterion of the spirit of their times.

As characteristic of the spirit of the civilization of the nineteenth century, I described the insane competition, where a man in a foul fight must "cheat, overreach, supplant, defraud, buy below worth and sell above, break down the business by which his neighbor fed his young ones, tempt men to buy what they ought not and to sell what they should not, grind their laborers, sweat their debtors, cozen their creditors,"*) in order to be able to support those dependent on him. I showed "that there had been many a man among the people of the nineteenth century who, if it had been merely a question of his own life would sooner have given it up than nourished it by bread snatched from others."†) I pictured the consequences of this insane and annihilating competition as a constant wear on the brains and bodies of the past generation, intensified by the permanent fear of poverty. The spectre of uncertainty walked constantly beside the man of the nineteenth century, sat at his table and went to bed with him, even whispering in his ears: "Do your work ever so well, rise early and toil till late, rob cunningly or serve faithfully, you shall never know security.

---

*) Such parts of Mr. Bellamy's book as are characteristic of his manner of dealing with the present and with the future, I give with marks of quotation, adding in a foot note the page of " Looking Backward," where the sentence may be found. The above remarks are taken from page 277.

†) Page 277.

Rich you may be now and still come to poverty at last. Leave ever so much wealth to your children, you can not buy the assurance, that your son may not be the servant of your servant or that your daughter will not sell herself for bread."**)

And while one hundred and thirteen years ago all men worked like slaves, until completely exhausted, without having even a guaranty that they would not die in poverty or from hunger, the men of the twentieth century were walking in the sunlight of freedom, security, happiness and equality. After receiving an excellent education in standard schools and then passing through an apprenticeship of three years, the young people of the twentieth century select their vocation. Short hours of work permit them, even during the years of service in the industrial army, to spend more time for the continuation of their studies and for recreation than the people who lived a hundred years ago had ever believed to be consistent with a successful management of industries, farming or public affairs.

Free from all cares, in perfect harmony with each other, without the disturbing influence of political parties, enjoying a wealth unprecedented in the history of nations, we might verily say: "The long and weary winter of our race is ended. Its summer has begun. Humanity has burst the chrysalis. The heavens are before it!"††)

**) Page 321.
††) Page 292.

I had spoken with enthusiasm, yes, even with deep emotion and I expected, if not a warm, at least a sympathetic reception of my address. But only a faint and very cold applause followed my remarks. I had the impression that not one fourth of the young men present had found it worth their while to show their approval of my lecture, and that the applause of even these few had been an act of courtesy rather than a spontaneous outburst of feeling. The chilly reception was such a great disappointment to me that I could not rally courage enough to leave my chair and pass through the students as they were leaving the hall.

I busied myself at the little desk before me until everybody had gone with the exception of the gentleman who had arrested my attention when I entered the room. He remained at the door evidently waiting for me.

"You belong to the college?" I asked, to hide my embarrassment.

"Indeed I do", he answered with a light smile, that challenged another question.

"I suppose I have the pleasure of meeting one of my colleagues", I continued. "My name is West".

"Until about a month ago I was Professor Forest, your predecessor in teaching the history of the nineteenth century ; to-day I am one of the janitors and my chief has been good enough to recommend this room to my care."

I had during the last few days seen and heard so

many new and strange things, that I was prepared to be surprised at nothing, however astounding.

But the information, that to a professor of history was assigned the duty of cleaning the rooms, where he had once lectured, sounded so incredible and opened such an unpleasing prospect for my own career, that I could not conceal my amazement.

"And what has caused this singular change of position", I inquired.

"In comparing the lot of humanity in 1900 and 2000 I came to conclusions very different from yours", responded Mr. Forest.

"You do not mean to say, that the condition of the people of the nineteenth century was better than that of the present generation?" I asked with some curiosity.

"That is my opinion", said Mr. Forest.

"The only way I can understand you holding such extraordinary views, is that you are personally quite unacquainted with the civilization of which you speak so highly," I declared.

"I have a as matter of course, drawn my information from our libraries, and I am forced to admit that you can support your argument in regard to the civilization of the last century by pointing to your personal knowledge. But I am afraid that you are not so familiar with the present state of affairs, at the fountain of your information in regard to the twentieth century is only one man, Dr. Leete. I may therefore claim that my information of the civilization of your days is better than yours of our institutions, because mine is based on the testimony of more witnesses than one."

"Then you must of course disapprove the views developed in my lecture?"

"Your address will undoubtedly be published in extenso in all the administration organs, that is, in nearly every newspaper in the land", said Mr. Forest, evading a direct answer to my question.

"Administration organs you say", I asked with surprise: "Has the administration organs, and why does it need them?"

"Of course the administration has organs", answered Forest. "And it is both difficult and unpleasant to edit an opposition paper. Therefore we have only a few of them."

"But Dr. Leete said: "We have no parties or politicians and as for demagoguery and corruption, they are words having only a historical significance."*) And yet you speak of opposition and of administration papers?" I said this very likely with an expression of some doubt in my eyes.

My companion broke into a loud laugh, after which he asked: "Excuse, please, my merriment, but Dr. Leete is a great joker, who never fails to "bring down the house." Well! Well! That is too good. I wish I could have seen his face when he gave you that information."

And Mr. Forest laughed again.

*) Page 60.

"I beg your pardon, Mr. West", he continued, when I met his merriment with silence; "but you would not only excuse but share my laughter, if you were familiar with our public life, if you knew Dr. Leete as well as I do and then learned that he had claimed, we were suffering from a want of politicians. But I wish to say right here", added Mr. Forest in a more composed tone, "that I have not a poor opinion of Dr. Leete. He is a practical joker, a shrewd politician, but otherwise as good a man as our time can produce."

"Dr. Leete is a politician?" I asked in the utmost astonishment.

"Yes. Dr. Leete is the most influential leader of the administration party in Boston. I owe it to his kind interference, that I am still connected with the college."

Noticing that I did not know how to construe this statement, Mr. Forest added:

"When, in comparing the civilization of your days with ours, I came to the conclusion, that communism had proved a failure, I was accused of misleading and corrupting the students and the usual sentence in such cases: "confinement in an insane asylum", was passed. Because, it is claimed, that only a madman could find fault with the best organization of society ever introduced. Dr. Leete, however, declared, that my insanity was so harmless, that confinement in an asylum seemed unnecessary, besides being too expensive. I could still earn my living by doing light work about the college building; and my case would serve as a warning to all the professors and students to be careful.in their expressions and teachings. So I retained the liberty in which we glory and was spared doing street cleaning or some such work, which is generally awarded to "kickers" against the administration."

"The students seem to share your opinion, at least they received my remarks very coldly," I remarked, in order to avoid a discussion of the qualities of my host.

Mr. Forest's keen grey eyes rested for a moment upon my face, and then he said in a friendly tone:

"I believe you were convinced of what you said, Mr. West; but did it not occur to you, that you treated your time and your contemporaries very severely? Did competition really demand, that one should defraud his neighbor, grind his laborers, sweat his debtors and snatch the bread from others? Were the majority of the men of your time swindlers and Shylocks? Were the laborers all slaves, working each day until completely exhausted? I remember distinctly, that the wage-workers of your time struck frequently for eight hours, declining to work nine or ten hours per diem for good pay. I think you had a strong, proud and independent class of laborers, who could not fairly be regarded as slaves. And as for the girls, I have seen the statements and complaints, that help for housekeeping was very scarce in your days and was paid from $2. to $5. per week, with board, so that there was no excuse for any decent girl to sell herself for bread.— Of course your state of civilization was very far from being faultless; in fact there is no such thing as perfection in anything. But your description of the civilization of the nineteenth century is painted in such dark colors, that our students, who are somewhat familiar with the history of those days, could not very well enthuse over your lecture; especially as many of these young men do not regard our present institutions with such complete admiration as you do. I speak frankly, Mr. West, and I hope you will excuse my frankness, because of my desire to serve you in describing men, things and institutions as I see them."

The warm tone of his voice and the sympathetic expression of his eyes caused me to shake hands with Forest, although everything he had said went directly against my friends, my views, my feelings and my interests. I left him in an uneasy mood and walked home revolving in my mind his criticism of my lecture.

I met Dr. Leete and the ladies, and Edith inquired whether my debut as professor had satisfied my expectations.

I have always tried to be frank and true : so I gave Dr. Leete and his family a synopsis of my speech, mentioned the cool reception of my address and my disappointment. I spoke of Mr. Forest's criticism, leaving out, of course, his observations relative to Dr. Leete, and confessed that his censure was not wholly undeserved inasmuch as I had gone too far in charging upon the whole people the bad qualities which reckless competition had stamped on certain individuals.

Dr. Leete was evidently not altogether pleased with
my remarks. After a short pause he said: "I think
the reckless competition of the last part of the nineteenth century could not fail to demoralize more or
less, in most cases more, all the people, who were
conducting a business or who had to work for a living. I think furthermore that your lecture was an
excellent exposition of principles and that you have
no reason to yield an inch of your position. The
cold reception you met with, ought not to worry you.
It is due to Forest, who has planted in the hearts of
our students his idiosyncrasy, his blind admiration of
competition and his aversion to our form of civilization. It is your task to enlighten the young men in
regard to the comparative merits of the two orders of
things. — Mr. Forest is placing a heavy tax on the
patience of his fellow citizens by his persistent efforts
to mislead the students. — Did he mention the fact
that he was your predecessor?"

"He did, when I asked him if he were a member of
the college staff of teachers. He said that he was
discharged for his heresy and that he owed his comparatively lenient treatment to you."

"It is not Forest's habit to conceal his opinions
and he may have given you a nice idea of Dr. Leete",
my host said with a smile.

I thought best under the circumstances to repeat
Forest's remarks in regard to Dr. Leete, which remarks
were very good natured and rather complimentary to
my host. I may add that I desired very much to

know what Dr. Leete would say in answer to the charge of being a politician and a leader of the administration party.

So I said: "Mr. Forest laughed heartily when I repeated your remarks that you have no party nor politicians. He called you a great practical joker, a shrewd politician, the leader of the administration party in Boston and a good man."

Dr. Leete smiled somewhat grimly as he replied: "That is a character I ought to be grateful for, considering that it comes from a faultfinder like Forest. Concerning his references to me as a politician I will say that I never held an office, but that the administration has occasionally consulted me and other citizens on important questions. Political parties we have not. There are of course a few incurable faultfinders like Mr. Forest and a few radical growlers, but we pay but little attention to them so long as they do not disturb the public peace. If they do, we send them to a hospital where they receive proper treatment."

Althoug.. these words were spoken in the tone of light conversation, they impressed me deeply. "If they do, we send them to a hospital, where they receive proper treatment." Did not this confirm Forest's statement, that the usual sentence against the opponents of communism was confinement in an insane asylum?"

My unpleasant thoughts were interrupted by Edith's sweet voice remarking: "I think Mr. Forest is an

honest well meaning gentleman and he should be permitted to express his views, even if they are wrong
and queer. The students will certainly eventually be
convinced that our order of things is as good as it
can be made, and besides it is so entertaining to hear
once in a while another opinion."

With an expression of fatherly love, Dr. Leete
placed his right hand on Edith's thick hair and said:
"The ladies of the court of Louis XVI. of France also
considered very entertaining the ideas that caused the
revolution and cost many of the "entertained" ladies
and gentlemen their heads beneath the guillotine. —
Ideas are little sparks. They may easily cause a
conflagration if not watched".

CHAPTER III.

My studies had never been directed to questions of national economy. I had never thought of comparing the merits of competition with those of com- . munism. When Dr. Leete had explained in his positive and still fascinating manner the new order of things I had hardly noticed that it was based on communistic principles. I thought humanity had reached at last the millennium, and when Dr. Leete stated that his easy and even luxurious way of living represented the average style of the people of the twentieth century, I had no doubt that everybod" was satisfied with the new order of things.

My cool reception by the students and my conversation with Mr. Forest had convinced me, that not every inhabitant of the United States in the 2000th year of our Lord considered the present order of things the millennium and I must say that I noticed the dissatisfaction with sincere sorrow. For a sweet peace, a tranquillity never felt before, had filled my heart, when Dr. Leete spoke of the absolute happiness of the men of the twentieth century.

My new profession imposed upon me the duty of studying national economy. Of course I could have pictured simply the social and political circumstances, in which the people of the United States had lived 113 years ago, but this would not have satisfied me. I desired to learn, how the civilizations of the two centuries, if impartially judged, would compare. Therefore I cultivated my acquaintance with Mr. Forest, to hear from him the arguments against the theories set forth by Dr. Leete, although a feeling of discomfort always overwhelmed me, whenever the thought came to me, that Forest's ideas might prove victorious over the principles advanced by Dr. Leete. For a victory won by Forest could mean nothing else but a return to a state of affairs, which I thoroughly disliked. and which I knew to be full of cares and discomforts.

I confined my next lecture to an accurate discription of the state of the labor market of Boston in 1887. Avoiding carefully all exaggerations, I drew only indisputable conclusions from the facts given, showing how capital and labor had lost equally by the numerous strikes in those days and complimenting the present order of things, for making such irrational economical conflicts impossible.

After my lectures I always conversed with Mr. Forest, who was quite as willing to discuss the new order of society as Dr. Leete.

"The friends of the administration are calling me a fault-finder", said Mr. Forest, "and they are right. although they might express their opinion with more civility, if they said, that I am critically disposed. I would criticise every administration under which it chanced to be my destiny to live, however good or bad that administration might be. I do not harbor any animosity against the men, who rule the United States to-day. I even admit that they exercise a little more wisdom, energy and tolerance, than did the members of the government, which ruled twelve years ago. But the fundamental principle of their system is decidedly wrong and so the consequences must be bad ; — whatever the members of the administration may do to patch up the shortcomings of their system".

"So you think that the present system is absolutely wrong ?" I queried.

"Can you entertain any doubts ?" answered Forest. "Look around! Is the leading principle in creation equality or variety ? You find sometimes similitude but never conformity. Botanists have carefully compared thousands of leaves, which looked exactly alike at the first glance, but which after close examination were found to possess striking dissimilarities. Inequality is the law of nature and the attempt to establish equality is therefore unnatural and absurd. Whereever such experiments have been made, they have ended in unqualified failure. Even some of the first Christians, moved by brotherly love and charity, failed in their efforts to establish communism permanently. And the lamented Procrustes used two bedsteads in which he placed his victims. He could not get along with one size for everybody. We may just as well try to make every man six feet long, forty-two inches around his chest, with a Grecian nose, blue

eyes, light hair and a lyric tenor voice, as to attempt
to equalize all lives and reduce them to a communistic
state.—Now consider, in connection with the differ-
ence in the mental and physical powers of men, their
different inclinations and tastes, the variety of their
occupations, and then say, whether the establishment
of society on the basis of communism, of absolute
equality, is possible."

"If I have formed a just appreciation of the organization of your society, you have recognized the right
of all men to a living by giving everybody an equal
share of the products of labor", I objected; "but at
the same time you give everybody the chance to
select the profession or trade most to his taste and
you have graded the men, belonging to a guild, thus
inciting the ambition of the worker, to reach a higher
grade, and creating a diversity of positions, adapted
to that disimilarity of men, you were just speaking
of".

"Yes", said Forest, "we first established the principle
of equality and then proceeded to arrange our system
upon a basis of inequality, thus avoiding an open
avowal that the new organization of society was a
failure in both theory and practice. The question
before us is a very plain one: *"Are we all alike"?* If
we are, then communism is the proper form of society
and everybody should have an equal share of the
products of labor. If we are not alike, if we differ
in mental power and in physical ability, if the results
of the labor of men are different, then there is no
reason, why the wealth of the nation should be

equally divided. But we first proclaim equality and pretend that we divide the products of labor equally among all; and then we divide the "workers into *first, second* and *third grades*, according to *ability*, and these grades are *subdivided* into *first* and *second classes.*"*) Here we see the workers subdivided into six classes for the reason, expressly stated, that their ability *differs*. That their diligence also differs is not admitted, but it is nevertheless the fact. The *inequality* of men is thus *distinctly recognized*, but the products of labor are *equally* divided in the name of *equality!* Now, everybody has a natural right to the products of his activity, but we are taking a large share of the results of the labor of a clever worker of class A of the first grade to give it to a lazy fellow of class B of the third grade. This is downright robbery, not even hidden beneath the shabby cloak of the leading principle governing all the acts of the administration ; and all those who can not admire this stealing, are denounced as enemies of the best organization of society, ever known in the history of mankind".

"You are to a certain extent an admirer of the civilization of the nineteenth century", I answered ; "and yet in our times the employers were accused by some of the labor agitators of "stealing" a large amount of the products of work by reaping very large profits and paying small wages. I would rather favor an equal division of all properties than a

*) Page 125.

system, by which a comparatively small number of employers can enrich themselves at the expense of the masses of the laboring people."

"I am not an admirer of the civilzation of the nine-teenth century, Mr. West," Forest exclaimed. "I simply maintain, that the principles of *competition* under which society worked a hundred years ago was far *superior* to the *communism*, under which we are laboring. The unjust profits of the employers, of which you complain, could have been easily done away with, if your workmen had organized themselves into co-partnerships or associations. There was no law a hundred years ago to prevent a dozen shoe-makers renting a loft with steam power, purchasing a few sewing and other machines and making boots and shoes at their own risk. There was no law to prevent all the other workingmen buying their boots and shoes at the shop of the co-operative association, thus securing for the members of the latter the profits of the manufacturer, wholesaler, retailer and work-man. The laborers of all the different trades had a perfect right to organize such co-operative societies and thus secure all the profit that was in their labor. If the workmen preferred not to make use of this chance, if they did not care to assume the cares and risks of conducting a business for themselves, if they would rather work for an employer, leaving the cares and risks of the managements entirely to him, they had certainly no reason to complain of the profit of the employer. And if they were not satisfied with their treatment they could at any time seek other employment ; — a thing that the workmen of our days *can not do,* for there is only one employer, the national administration. — The principle, that a man has a right to what he produces, was not questioned under your form of production. But we have in the name of equality and justice established the "right" to rob an industrious man of a part of the product of his labor and give this booty to his lazy comrade. If the workingmen of the nineteenth century, instead of sacrificing enormous sums in strikes, had organized one trade after another into co-operative associations, they would have solved what they styled the social questions with comparatively little trouble. And they would have saved us from the present outrageous form of society."

"The strikes were an effect merely of the concentration of capital in greater masses, than had ever been known before", I said, repeating the views of Dr. Leete on this question. "Before this concentration began.... the individual workman was relatively important and independent in his relations to his employers. Moreover, when a little capital or a new idea was enough to start a man in business for himself, workingmen were constantly becoming employers and there was no hard or fast line between the two classes. Labor unions were needless then and general strikes out of the question".*)

*) Page 52.

"In your place, Mr. West, I would not endorse those sentences of Dr. Leete", said Forest with a smile, "for the Doctor has had frequent occasions to change his mind on this subject and persists in repeating his erroneous statements, although I and others have disproved them until further repetitions of our arguments became tedious. Strikes are not, as Dr. Leete pretends to believe, comparatively late appearances on the battle fields of national economy. One of the biggest strikes that ever occurred, the "secessio in montem sacrum", took place in Rome as early as 494 before Christ, and, during the centuries of the middle ages, strikes for higher wages frequently occurred, although in those days labor was much better organized (in trades unions, guilds and "Zuenfte") and more powerful than capital. And as for the impossibility of laborers ever becoming employers, I can show you in the college library a copy of the German paper, the "Freie Presse", published in the city of Chicago anno 1888, where the editor, in contradicting similar statements of the communists of those days, points to the fact, that in 1888 there were 12,000 German house owners, manufacturers and well to do or rich business men in Chicago, who all had come to the city poor. When these Germans came to Chicago only a very few of them spoke English, still they were able to acumulate fortunes. This disproves the statement, that the people at the end of the last century were in the clutches of capi tal and unable to free themselves. — It is the easiest thing in the world to make wild statements, but it is sometimes difficult to substantiate them. And Dr. Leete is an adapt at making statements".

"But are you not getting along in good style?" I asked, hoping to stop Forest's complaints, by pointing to an undisputable fact. "Are you not enjoying an unprecedented prosperity and is not this general result, the definite annihilation of poverty, an achievement worth small sacrifices ? "

"We are not getting along in good style. We are not enjoying an unprecedented prosperity. You will discover very soon, that you are overestimating the character and the fruits of our civilization. And so far as the annihilation of poverty is concerned, it amounts practically to nothing but the enrichment of the awkward, stupid and lazy people, with the proceeds of the work of the clever and industrious women and men. You could have done that 113 years ago, but you were not foolish and unjust enough to commit such a robbery."

"If the people don't like the present organization of society, why do they not change it?" I asked. "From your remarks, I have drawn the conclusion, that you have no opposition party worth speaking of, for you said, there are only a few opposition papers published in the country. This seems to prove that the people are satisfied with the present state of affairs".

Forest looked very severe as he answered: "You are of course under the impression, that we are acting with the same liberty you were enjoying 113 years ago. But everything in political life has changed since those days. With the exception of a limited number of government officials and a few contractors, your citizens were perfectly independent of the administration ; to-day the administration rules everything, and everybody is more or less dependent upon the good will of our rulers. Whoever dares to openly oppose the ruling spirits may be sure that all the wrath and all the unpleasantness at the command of the administration, will be piled upon him and his relatives and friends. Therefore the number of men who are daring enough to challenge the ire of the government is very small, although a great many are discontented with the present state of affairs."

"But why don't people elect men to congress, who would pass laws, that would change a state of things, so unsatisfactory to the masses?" I asked, satisfied, that Forest in his fault-finding mood, was using his dark paint altogether to freely.

"Congress has very little influence nowadays", Forest answered. "The power rests almost entirely with the president and the chiefs of the ten great departments. They have well nigh absolute power and resemble somewhat the council of ten in Venice, when that aristocratic Republic was at the height of its power. As it lies within their discretion to assign each and every person to a good or a poor position for twenty-four years and even to order a draft from the ranks of the men over forty-five years of age, thus being able to get disliked men back under the direct discipline of the industrial army, they have a power over all the people that no tyrant of your times ever dreamed of establishing".

"You know of course", Mr. Forest continued, "that all recruits belong for the first three years of their service to the class of unskilled or common laborers. It is not until after this period, during which he is *assignable* to *any work* at the *discretion of his superiors*, that the young man is allowed to select a special avocation".*)   You can readily see that the young man is during these three years at the absolute mercy of his superiors. They may assign him to easy and clean work, or they may send him to do a dirty and unhealthy job.   He has to obey orders.   For "a man able to do duty and persistently refusing, is sentenced to solitary imprisonment on bread and water until he consents".†)

"You know furthermore, that "individual *records are kept* and that excellence receives distinction, corresponding with the penalties that negligence incurs." Dr. Leete has undoubtedly told you this and furthermore "that it is not policy with us to permit youthful recklessness or indiscretion, when not deeply culpable, to handicap the future careers of young men and that all who have passed the unclassified grade without serious disgrace, have an equal opportunity to choose the life employment they have the

*) Page 70.
†) Page 128.

most liking for . . . . Now not only are the individual records of these apprentices for ability and industry strictly kept and excellency distinguished by suitable distinctions, but upon the average of his record during his apprenticeship the standing given the apprentice among the full workmen depends. . . .*) While the internal organizations of the various industries, mechanical and agricultural, differ according to their peculiar conditions, they agree in a general division of their workers into first, second and third grades, according to ability, and these grades are in many cases subdivided into first and second classes. According to his *standing* as an *apprentice*, a young man is *assigned* his place as a *first, second* or *third grade worker. Regradings take place* in each industry at intervals, corresponding with the length of the apprenticeship. . . . One of the notable advantages of a high grading, is the *privilege* it gives the worker to select which of the various branches or processes of his industry he will follow as his specialty"†). . . . Dr. Leete has of course further informed you, "that so far as possible, the preferences of the poorest workman are considered in assigning him his line of work. . . . While however the wish of the lower grade man is consulted so far as the exigencies of the service permit, he is considered only after the upper grade men are provided for, and often he has to put up with second or third choice or even

*) Page 124.

†) Page 125.

with an *arbitrary assignment* when help is needed.
This privilege of selection attends every *regrading*,
and when a man loses his grade, he also risks having
to exchange the sort of work he likes best for some
other less to his taste.... High places in the nation
are open only to the highest class men."*)

These regulations bear out what I just said in regard
to the power of the administration. The lieutenants,
captains and colonels, are appointed by the generals
of the guild, who in turn are under the command of
the ten chiefs of the ten great departments. These
officers may give their young friends, who enter the
industrial army as apprentices, easy jobs and good
records and enable their friends on the strength of
their records, as soon as they have passed the first
three years of service, to enter the first class of the
first grade of a trade. And such a favorite, who,
backed by influential friends, has passed an easy time
as an apprentice and who has received at once the
first class of the first grade of his trade is immediately
appointable to a lieutenantship and he can run up to
the higher honors in a few years. — You can not deny,
Mr. West, that our regulations permit such a favoritism."

I had to admit that such things were possible.

Mr. Forest continued: "On the other hand, the
young men, who are not the sons and friends of our
leaders, are fortunate if they can secure a second
grade position, with a record, that does not exclude

*) Pages 125 and 126.

all hopes of further promotion. Relatives of out-
spoken opponents of the administration, can be
placed in the second class of the third grade of their
trade, and their record can be so kept, that they can
never hope to secure a higher position. And such a
favoritism is not only possible, but it absolutely does
exist. The sons and relatives of men, who are known
as opponents of the administration, have practically
to live worse than slaves, and are sometimes treated
like foot balls".

"Is there no court of appeals?" I asked.

"Yes, such an abused man or woman can go to a
Judge", Mr. Forest answered. "But, the minor Judges
are merely men who have passed the 45th year of age
and have been appointed to such a position for five
years by the president. They — as Dr. Leete of
course told you—adjudicate all cases where a member
of the industrial army makes a complaint of unfair-
ness against an officer. All such questions are *heard*
and settled without appeal by a single Judge, three
Judges being required only in graver cases. The
efficiency of industry requires the *strictest discipline*
in the army of labor"*)— The men appointed by the
President are of course trustworthy friends of the
administration and not expected to decide in such
cases against the officers of the government and in
favor of the "Kickers". And as such cases are
settled without appeal, the ill-used member of the
industrial army has to go back to his old position,

*) Page 206.

where the superior, whom he has accused, will certainly not treat him better than before. On the contrary, such an officer has a first-class chance to "get even" with his dissatisfied subordinate, especially at the next regrading, when he can put him into the last class and grade, if the unfortunate fellow is not already there. If such is the case, the offended officer can at least assign the "Kicker" to the most objectionable work".

The picture, thus drawn by Mr. Forest, appeared so dreadful, especially when compared by me with the descriptions of Dr. Leeté, that I could not collect myself sufficiently to try an argument against the conclusions of my predecessor in the professorship of the history of the nineteenth century..

After a short pause the present janitor continued: "Now consider in connection with all the facts and institutions that I have mentioned, that *"the workers have no suffrage to exercise or anything to say about the choice"* of their *superiors.**)—"The general of the guild appoints to the ranks under him, but he himself is not appointed, but chosen by suffrage among the superintendents by vote of the honorary members of the guilds, that is by those who have served their time in the guild and received their discharge"†). — So my dear Mr. West, the members of the industrial army are twenty-four years absolutely at the mercy of their superiors. If they desire to

*) Page 277.
†) Page 189.

have a good time they must blindly obey orders and seek favor by all means in their power. They must influence their friends who have votes not only to stand by the administration, but to do it in a demonstrative manner. Occasional presents of wines and cigars may secure the friendship of some of the officers. Otherwise the member of the industrial army may lead for twenty-four years a life, compared with which the lot of a plantation slave or of the poorest coal digger 150 years ago would be called an enviable fate. For a plantation slave was considered a valuable piece of property and not recklessly destroyed, while the poorest coal digger could leave his job and go to some other place, until he found more suitable employment. A member of our industrial army, who has drawn down upon himself the ire of the officers of the administration or who is placed on the list of the enemies of society on account of the opposition of his voting relatives, leads a life that may be termed as "twenty four years of hell on earth"! I have demonstrated to you now, Mr. West, why congress has no influence. The vast majority of its members are continually trying to please the administration, for the purpose of securing favors for themselves, their relatives and their friends," said Mr. Forest in conclusion. "And this is the equality of the best organization society ever had ; this is what Dr. Leete calls the millennium".

CHAPTER IV.

"It is in conformity with the laws of nature and, therefore, right that a man should push his son, his relatives and friends, and I would not blame a man for doing this ; I should rather denounce him for not doing it—always provided, of course, that said son, said relatives or friends were qualified to fill the positions to which they are appointed", said Mr. Forest at our next conversation. "I remember that I have read in certain books a great deal about the nepotism shown at your time in the distribution of the federal patronage, and that General Grant was accused of always preferring his relatives and friends in making appointments. I sympathize with that great commander in the sturdiness with which he stood by his friends, and I am inclined to excuse the mistakes, he sometimes made in his appointments, because they were mistakes of his heart that was always true to his friends and sometimes was inclined to overestimate their ability, or sense of honor. If the ties of blood and friendship are not to be considered, what else should be ? And since a man is bound to know the character and ability of his relatives and friends better than the qualities of other people, he should certainly first appoint those next to him to positions for which they are qualified."

"But the trouble with our political and social system is, that it is bound to breed not only favoritism, but also corruption on the largest scale. One hundred and thirteen years ago, the men at the head of the National Government or those who were influential with them were also sometimes filling places, where for little work a good salary was paid, with unworthy women and men, but such sinecures were comparatively few and far between. The number of federal officials in your days was, if I am not mistaken about 80,000, and the postmasters of the small country towns, who made up the largest part of the 80,000 were paid such a beggarly commission for the sale of postage stamps, that no one could afford to accept such positions except trades people, who kept a store, where they had to be all day anyhow, and to whom the honor and small profits were an object. And then the incumbents of all the offices that could be classed as sinecures, were changed every four or eight years. Our administrations have a very long life. The one ousted twelve years ago lasted twenty-six years. And the number of positions at the command of the government is very large. There is one lieutenant or overseer to about each and every twelve men or women, not to mention the captains, colonels, etc. ; and the amount of bookkeeping done, is simply enormous. We are keeping books as you know, I suppose, in all the producing as well as in the distribu-

ting departments, and more than that: every citizen
has an account in the police books*).

"When you take into consideration our great and
growing population, you can form some idea of how
enormous this work is. You are aware, that the
North American territory, formerly under British rule,
has been annexed to the United States, and that the
population, according to the census of 1990, numbered
414,000,000. It is now estimated at 500,000,000**).
The complicated system of bookkeeping required by
the communistic plan of production, and the short-
ness of working hours granted to the bookkeepers,
who are all preferred men and women, favorites of
the members of the administration, made it necessary
to appoint a bookkeeper for every fifty people. Under the former administration we had one bookkeeper
for every forty-two people. This gives to the government a chance to provide, at its own pleasure,
over 10,000,000 of men and women with clean and
easy work. Add to these 10,000,000 of positions about
10,000,000 officers of the industrial army, from the
lieutenantships up to the positions of colonel ; add,
furthermore, the clerkships in the distributing places'

*) Page 87.

**) The first census of the United States was taken in 1790,
when 3,929,314 people were counted. In 1880 the population
numbered 50,155,738, and in 1890 it is about 68,000,000. In one
hundred years it has been multiplied by 16. If the rate of increase
should continue to be the same, the United States would have in
1990, without the population of Canada, about 1,040,000,000 of
people. I have figured an increase of about twenty percent for
each decade, which would give for the year 2000 about 500
millions of inhabitants for the United States and Canada.

and many other preferred positions, and you can see at a glance what an enormous power the administration possesses and how tempting this power is."

"But is it not necessary for those applying for the responsible position of a bookkeeper to have passed through a course of study in order to be qualified for such important duties?" I inquired.

"Bookkeeping is part of the instruction in our schools", Mr. Forest answered, "and the bookkeeping in the public offices is not well done. So the responsibility, resting on the shoulders of the favorites of the members of the administration, does not harass the minds of these preferred people very much. It is, of course, impossible for an outsider to obtain an insight into the workings of the present administration, and to know how the books are kept. But when the late administration went out of office twelve years ago, an unfathomable pool of corruption was uncovered. An inventory of the goods on hand was taken, and it was stated that the books showed a shortage of more than four hundred and thirty-two million dollars. The members of the ousted administration declared this statement to be entirely false, that it had been "doctored" by the experts of the administration, for the purpose of casting discredit upon the members of the old government. The accused officers admitted that shortages were possible, for the reason, that all the clerks whose duty it was to measure goods, were inclined to give the people good weight and large measure, but that these shortages would not reach the figure of $432,000,000, and that the deficiency could not be considered as a proof of want of honesty on the part of the old officers. On the other hand, the new officers claimed, that the enormous shortages were due to the corruption of the members and prominent supporters of the ousted administration, who had always overdrawn their accounts, and had not been charged with the goods taken out in excess of their credit cards".

I asked Mr. Forest what he thought of these charges.

"I think, they were to a large extent well founded. The temptation under our wretched system is too great. That the leaders should give to their relatives and next friends good positions would not be blame-worthy, if the appointees were fit to fill the places given them. But the best places, numbering in all about twenty millions, are not filled with the best and most able men. They go, so far as they are not given to the relatives and friends of the leaders, to friends of the administration, in order to keep the latter in power. They are given to the sons and relatives and friends of the most active supporters of the govern-ment. And even this would be tolerable, if the favoritism stopped there, at the boundary of corrup-tion and tyranny. But it does not".

"Are you accusing the present administration and all its friends of corruption and tyranny?" I asked, feeling that I should have to end my conversations with Mr. Forest, if he should make disparaging charges, even indirectly, against my host.

"I am speaking of a system and I am mentioning only such facts and deeds as I can prove", Mr. Forest answered. "I am not accusing men for any pleasure it gives me to do so. I know that your question refers to Dr. Leete and, though it is not a direct one, yet I will meet it squarely. I regard Dr. Leete as one of the best and purest of men among the party-leaders; but he, also, is making use of the advantages that our system offers to the men in power."

"Will you be kind enough to substantiate what you say?" I asked quietly, but sharply.

"I will leave it to you to say, whether I am going too far in my statement", Forest continued. "Did not Dr. Leete inform you that he has been "cherishing the idea of building a laboratory in the large garden of his house?"*) And did he not tell you that he sent for the workmen and that they unearthed the vault in which you slept?"†)

"Indeed, Dr. Leete said that he intended to build a chemical laboratory", I admitted; "but is not the amount of his credit-card large enough to permit him such an expenditure?"

Forest looked somewhat amused and asked me, if I had ever looked at the total amount the credit-card called for. I confessed that I never had; noticing that the style of living of Dr. Leete was luxurious

*) Page 34.
†) Page 34.

enough for anybody, I had not troubled myself to ascertain how much the country allowed each and every inhabitant per year.

"Well", said Mr. Forest, "we will discuss the wealth of the nation at some other time   To-day we will continue to investigate the tendency of the communistic system to breed favoritism, corruption, servility and suppression of opponents. — As for Dr. Leete, he is building his laboratory in spite of the fact, that such an enterprise is entirely against the intention and spirit of our institutions.   There is a very good laboratory of the kind in the basement of this college, and Dr. Leete would certainly be welcome, if he should ask permission to experiment there at his pleasure. His influence, if nothing else, would secure him a permit.   But vanity causes him to erect a superfluous building, which will give the Radicals a new and visible argument against the ruling clique".

"What Radicals are you speaking of?" I asked.

"I am refering to the radical communists who object to the present state of affairs, because they desire to abolish religious services, matrimony and all personal-property, institutions that are at present tolerated.   We will speak of our political parties and their principles later.   I simply desired to establish to your own satisfaction, or dissatisfaction, the fact, that Dr. Leete is erecting for his private use and in violation of communistic principles, a chemical laboratory, a very expensive affair, for which the credit-cards of ten men would not pay, and thus challenging the criticism of all the enemies of the administration".

"Cannot Dr. Leete pay a fair rent for the laboratory?" I rejoined. "I should think that the abundance of labor could not be used to a better advantage than to erect buildings, the rent for which will increase the income of the nation".

"But there is no abundance of labor, as you will discover in due time", said Forest. "And if you will imagine what would happen, if every citizen should demand a similar outlay of labor and instruments to please his notions, you will undoubtedly see, that Dr. Leete is assuming an exceptional position, which, not only savors of favoritism but, also, involves an indiscreet abuse of power, calculated to create bad blood".

I could not very well refute the arguments of Mr. Forest, and so was silent.

"But favoritism and the occasional abuse of power for the accommodation of men like Dr. Leete, are not the worst features of our present form of government", he continued, "and the fact that influential men frequently receive presents of silks, furs, and jewelry for their wives and daughters, and of wine and cigars for themselves, from people seeking the intercession of these powerful men, in order to procure preferred positions for themselves or for relatives and friends, could also be borne although, of course, they are proofs of political corruption. But the worst consequences of this damnable communism are tyranny and the possibility of brutal persecution

of the opponents of the administration on the one
hand, and servility, adulation and calumny on the
other. Every man and every body of men who have
gained certain advantages or occupy desired positions will defend themselves against all attacks of
their opponents. So will political parties try to keep
themselves in power by rewarding their faithful workers and by crowding back their opponents. It is,
therefore, very dangerous to invest a great government with arbitrary powers, which permit the rulers
to make the people dependent upon the good will of
their officers, even in their daily occupation, all their
life long".

"According to your description the present state of
society appears to be an unbearable condition of
affairs", I said.

"If you inquire among the members of the different
guilds, especially among the farmers," Mr. Forest
continued, "you will find that I am describing things
just as they are. Every member of the industrial
army knows that ability and industry alone will secure
a desirable position only in exceptional cases, if at
all ; that political influence is. the almighty factor in
every affair of our lives, and that the industrial army
is governed by officers whom the worker must try to
please, by personal adulation, by presents, by a slav-
ish devotion to the orders of the superiors, and
indirectly by inducing all the members of his family
and all his friends to support every measure and
every member of the administration. If the mem-

bers of the industrial army could elect their officers, the discipline would of course, not be so strict, as it is now ; but even an occasional row amongst the men would be preferable to the present state of affairs, where every one who happens to be unpopular with the ruling party is leading a terrible existence. The number of suicides is therefore becoming larger every year and is to-day four times greater than in your times".

"The number of suicides in European armies 113 years ago was very large", I remarked thoughtfully, "although the men had everything they needed in the line of lodging, food and clothing".

"Yes," said Forest, "the necessities of life without liberty are of little value. The soldiers of your time threw away their lives, because they did not consider a life without freedom worth living, and still their term of service lasted only three or five years, and they had but a comparatively easy duty to perform in times of peace. The service in our industrial army lasts, at the best, 24 years of our life. The men and women are at the mercy of their officers, and they can appeal against maltreatment to other members of the administration only to judges who decide definitely such cases, generally by simply sending back the complainants to their work with an admonishment to try to win the good will of their superiors, and thus secure promotion."

"You have been speaking about politicians, Mr. Forest", I said "Do many men take an active part in political life?"

"I should say they did", my predecessor answered. "Many of the men from 45 years upwards, and many women do little else, except busy themselves with politics. They can live on their credit-cards wherever they please, and many of them prefer to spend their time in Washington, "hustling around" in a very lively fashion, trying to gain favors for their friends, and for such people as address themselves to the hustlers. The lobby in the halls of Congress in your days is described as a bad crowd, but to compare it with the hustlers of our days, would be like comparing a Sunday school with pandemonium. Millions of people who desire better work or promotion, and who have nothing to hope from the influence they are able to command at home, write to the hustlers at Washington to secure their services."

"But what can the seekers of favors offer to those who live in Washington for the purpose of gaining favor for other people, and whom we may call the lobbyists of the twentieth century?" I inquired. "In the present day, men do not accumulate fortunes."

"Indeed, they do not", answered Mr. Forest with a smile. "But some people desire to have occasionally a "high time" and to spend five or ten times the amount of their credit-card during each year. Some of our administration leaders keep, what we may style, a "great house". They receive guests and entertain them with delicacies and wine. Some of the most prominent lobbyists do the same thing. An applicant for favors has to give up a part or perhaps nearly all of his credit-card, and he may look to his future subordinates for a rich compensation".

"But why are people not satisfied with their legitimate income"? I asked, painfully surprised to see that wire-pulling and corruption were quite as prevalent as they had been 113 years ago. "Is not the income a credit-card affords sufficient to support people?"

"You can never satisfy the people", Forest said. "Nowadays the clever and industrious part of the people feel that they are robbed for the benefit of their lazy, awkward or stupid comrades, that they have to submit to the impudence and blackmailing of some of their superiors, or else undergo humiliating treatment. And even the men and women of the lowest ability, who are benefited by our present system, are not all of them pleased. Some of them would rather do away with personal property and separate housekeeping. In fact, but a very small portion of our citizens are really satisfied. — And people who are fond of good cooking, costly meals and Havana cigars, certainly cannot pay for such luxuries, and have to depend upon others if they desire to enjoy them. We have in Washington, also, a great many young women, who prefer flirtation, fine meals and a fast life to the regular employment in the industrial army or the life of an ordinary good wife".

"Then prostitution still flourishes in Washington", I exclaimed with amazement.

"Indeed it does", Mr. Forest assented. "Of course, these girls hold clerical positions in the different departments, but these positions are sinecures. I understand from friends who have seen part of the secret life at the capitol, (and it is not so very secret either) that some of the higher officials spend fifty times the amount of their credit cards with these women. A part of their income is obtained from those seeking favors, who willy-nilly give up a part of their credit cards. Another part of the values squandered by influential persons, comes from the public storehouse, where only a small proportion of the value taken out by the influential people, is pricked from their credit cards by the clerks, who are fully aware what is expected of them, if they desire to retain their positions; for if they should treat the leaders of the ruling party like common laborers, they would be degraded to class B of their third grade. The glitter of corruption proves attractive to many men and women, as I have stated before, and the population of Washington, therefore, exceeds that of any other city on the American continent."

"But, I cannot understand, why the people tolerate such a corrupt and tyrannical government as you describe," I said, "and I am satisfied that your hypochondriac disposition is befogging somewhat the keenness of your eyesight and the clearness of your judgment."

"It is your own fault if you remain in doubt as to the perfect correctness of my statements", Mr. Forest said. "If you, for instance, should desire to take a vacation for the purpose of **giving** our rulers in

Washington one of your enthusiastic lectures, you will cheerfully be granted leave of absence from your duties as professor and will be received at the capitol in grand style. For the enthusiasm displayed by you for our institutions, as compared with the civilization of the nineteenth century, will pour water on the mill wheels of our administration. You will find the state of affairs precisely as I have described them to be, and by conversing with the rank and file of the supporters of the administration, you will find that they are upholding the present state for the reason that they despair of their ability to improve public affairs, and because they are afraid of a rule still worse, under the radicals".

"How could a state of public affairs be worse than the one you have pictured to me in your conversations", I exclaimed.

"Many people are afraid that the Radicals would prohibit marriages and would force free love with all its consequences upon the people. In fact, the radical newspapers – the only sheets that speak out boldly against the administration and strike from the shoulder — are denouncing religion, marriage, separate house-keeping and the limited amount of property people are permitted to own".

"But, how can the tone of the Radical press be reconciled with your statement that the administration is treating its opponents so badly"? I asked. "If it is the custom of the government to confine its opponents in insane asylums, why are the Radical newspapers permitted to advocate such abominable principles"?

Mr. Forest laughed and replied : "The Radical editors are favored exceptions. They are doing good service for the administration in scaring the mass of the people into submission. Whenever an election of generals of the guilds is near at hand, the Radical press is permitted to howl to the best ability of its editors. Then, a few days before the election, the administration organs copy extracts from the rabid and nonsensical utterances of such papers, and ask the people, if they desire that kind of government, urge the voters to stand by the administration which can, of course, not please everybody in all points, but which is the best any people on earth ever had, and so forth ad infinitum".

"Then the Radical editors are simply tolerated as bugbears, while the more moderate writers are not permitted to oppose the administration?"

"Exactly", rejoined Mr. Forest. "But I am afraid, the government is playing a very dangerous game. The Radicals are undoubtedly gaining ground and have amongst their followers very desperate men, who may at any time raise the black flag of destruction. If we had a free and independent people, the danger would not be so great. Then the masses of free men would rally to the defence of their beloved institutions. But as matters now stand, the masses are accustomed to submission under a rule of a minority, and the determined uprising of a body of desperate men would find but a comparatively small number of citizens ready to fight for the present order of things. And it will be a bad day for humanity, when the Radicals come into power".

"But, you said that about twelve years ago the government lost an election. That shows, that it can be beaten in a square fight, and you further said that the present rulers are better citizens than the men that formed the last administration".

"There is certainly some improvement, but it is nothing very remarkable. It amounted, in substance, to a change of men, but not to a change of system. Favoritism, corruption and prostitution have decreased somewhat, but they have not been stamped out. They still flourish. People who were very enthusiastic at the time of the election and hoped for a clean and popular administration, have now lost all confidence, that under the communistic rule there can be such a thing as a just government. In sub-stance, it has been, as I said, merely a change of personalities and, therefore, the confidence of the people in the prevailing system has been destroyed. Consequently, the change has actually done more harm than good. The strongest and most reliable element to-day in favor of good government is the farming population; but although the farmers are very numerous, they represent one guild only. They have but one general and one department chief, and are outvoted by the representatives of the other guilds. And on account of the opposition of the farmers to the administration they are not treated as well as the members of the other guilds".

"Do they not receive the same credit cards as other people"? I queried.

"They do, but they complain that they receive the poorest goods, and that their share of public improvements and benefits is comparatively small; and whenever there is a chance to discriminate against their representatives, that chance is not lost. The farmers would be the most reliable opponents to the Radicals, but the treatment they are receiving from the administration, has created so much dissatisfaction amongst the farming population, that we cannot count upon them in a fight for the maintainance of the present system or the present government. To give you an instance of the discrimination against the farmers, I will mention the erection of music halls, theatres and other places of evolution, recreation and amusement. It is, of course, impossible to build a theatre or a concert hall at every country crossroad, but the number of such public places erected in the cities is entirely out of proportion to those erected in the country towns and villages The administration relies for its support upon the city people, upon such guilds as are recruited from the population of the cities, and, therefore bends all its energies to benefitting them. Then there is another thing to be taken into account. The nation is frequently left with small lots of goods on its hands, through changes of taste, unseasonable weather and various other causes. These have to be disposed of at a sacrifice, and the loss charged up to the expenses of the business*). These goods the administration can dispose of at any time when it chooses to claim that the best prices can be realized. The members of the administration are also judges as to what goods are to be sold at a sacrifice. It has been charged by the representatives of the farming population that such of these goods as are of poor quality are largely given out to farmers, while other things that are in first-class condition are disposed of in the storehouses of the cities, at reduced prices, and that in such instances favoritism and corruption are coming in. I do not care to endorse all the complaints, our farmers make. They may lack foundation to a great extent, but they prove the existence of a deep dissatisfaction, and such charges could simply not be made if our administration were not clothed with power hitherto unheard of in the history of mankind. It is the system itself that breeds all these evils".

"Have you not, besides the radical and the administration parties, other organizations fighting for the control of the government"?

"We have the temperance people who have organized themselves; but they are simply striving within the administration party to secure the control of the government. The administration does not discriminate against the members of this organization. It

*) Page 186

gives them a chance to do their very best, but so far they have not succeeded in making much headway".

"I notice that you are not giving the present system of society much credit for anything done under its auspices. Don't you think that the abolition of absolute poverty, the elevation of all men and women to a standard at least nearly equal, is a great and priceless gain to humanity? I remember too well the inexpressible sufferings of some of the poor people of my days, and while I am not sufficiently familiar with the present state of society, to endorse or to contradict your statements, yet I prize the abolishment of poverty so high, that I still cling to the hope, in spite of your arguments to the contrary, that the present form of society and of production may overcome all the difficulties inseparable from all human efforts and institutions".

"My dear Mr. West, I am glad to see you using now in your last remarks in defense of communism the same arguments the defenders of the old form of production used against the communists of your days. This simply proves two facts, viz.: that nothing is perfect under God's sun, and that every form of government is forced to admit this. The abolition of absolute poverty could have been accomplished as I can and will prove later on, beyond a reasonable doubt, without a descent into communism and the terrible consequences of this worst system of production. The fact, that the members and the officers of the administration may, at their pleasure, treat the friends of their opponents, members of the industrial army, like slaves; that even the friends of the government's opponents who have gained comparatively good positions, can be placed in the second class of the third grade at the yearly regradings, and that favoritism is shown to all friends of the administration, has caused adulation, servility, calumny and corruption, and there was never a time in the history of the Saxon race when there were in public business and social life so little independence and manhood among the citizens. When two hundred and thirty years ago England tried to levy a tax upon tea, the Americans rose up in arms, because they would not permit the government to collect a tax unless it granted to the Americans representation in the parliament which imposed this tax. To-day the government controls the labor of all men and women for twenty-four long years, without giving the flower of the American people a chance to cast a vote, which shall shape the form and policy of the government in conformity with the wishes of those who produce the wealth of the nation. This state of slavery which never existed before in the history of.civilized nations, can not last many years longer. It will go down in an ocean of blood. For as the German poet Schiller says: Fear not outrages from free men; but tremble when slaves break their chains".

CHAPTER V.

From a heaven of peace and joy, from an ideal state inhabited by good people only, Forest had thrown me into a deep dark sea of pity and doubt.

Dr. Leete and his family noticed, of course, the disturbed state of my thoughts, and while the doctor was evidently waiting for me to bring about a discussion of the social problems, Edith was anxious to console me. She seemed to think that the strangeness of my surroundings and of my present position was depressing me.

I carefully avoided an explanation. I had resolved to continue the conversations with Mr. Forest, but to form a clear opinion of my own by examining into the actual state of things, and thus find if the real facts bore out the statements of Dr. Leete or those of Mr. Forest. Therefore on my way to and from the college I strolled along the streets and conversed with all the people I met. I noticed with some surprise that everybody was reserved, yes even shy, when I commenced to ask about the administration of public affairs, about the principles underlying our form of government, about the behavior of the officers, the management of the storehouses, and whether the people were satisfied and pleased, or not.

Hardly ever did I meet an expression either of cheerful contentment, or of decided dissatisfaction. Only a few Radicals expressed themselves in strong language against the present state of things and against the leaders of the country, and a few women said that they did not like the work in the factories at all. But, although people were very reserved in the expression of their feelings and thoughts, I became convinced that contentment is as rare a flower in the garden of communism as it was in the United States of 113 years ago. The abominable language used by the Radicals against the highest officers of the country could not, of course, convince me that the latter were guilty of the charges preferred. But I could not elicit from any other man or from any other women of the rank and file of the industrial army a defense of the accused men. They evidently did not care to antagonize anybody when they were not called upon by one of their superiors to stand by the administration.

Thus, I was forced to the conclusion, that communistic rule did not create the universal happiness I expected to find after my conversations with Dr. Leete. But I was inclined to think that people lived well enough, without great cares, neither on the one hand particularly content with their lot, nor on the other inclined to change their system of production. And it seemed to me that most of the people were rather dull and did not take much interest in anything. One day when I reached the house of Dr.

Leete after one of my promenades through the streets of Boston, as I entered the hall, I heard a very loud conversation in one of the rooms. The first words that arrested my attention, spoken in a deep voice, trembling with emotion, were: "Miss Edith has encouraged me to repeat my visits"·

"We are always glad to see you here, Mr. Fest", Dr. Leete replied. "We have all invited you."

"Yes, you have; but you understand very well what I mean", the deep voice continued. "I have called here so frequently and have to-day asked Miss Edith to become my wife, because your daughter has encouraged my hopes to win her love. And now I am coolly informed that I have made a great mistake, and I see my suspicion confirmed, that this Bostonian of the nineteenth century, dug out by you from his grave in your garden, is the man whom Miss Edith prefers to all others, even the one she encouraged until a few days ago".

"Mr. Fest, I wish you would represent the civilization of the twentieth century with more dignity when you are speaking of my daughter and of my guest", said Dr. Leete with some emotion in his voice.

"Of course, I must preserve my dignity when I have been fooled by a base flirtation for over a year, and make the discovery that the girl I love is to marry a man 143 years old, in preference to me", Mr. Fest said in deep bitterness and somewhat sneeringly.

"How can you utter such cruel and untrue words," Edith exclaimed with angry excitement". "Never has the thought entered my mind that your feelings toward me, your friend for over ten years, were anything but brotherly affection".

"It is time to end this conversation", interposed Dr. Leete, "after the explanations given, Mr. Fest undoubtedly feels, that our relations can not be continued".

"Of course, our relations can not be continued", cried Mr. Fest in a rage. "I leave you now, and give you, now and here, fair warning that I shall not enter your house again as a friend. If I ever come again, it will be as an enemy to be avenged for the destruction of my happiness and the peace of my heart. Beware of that day"!

The reckless manner in which this man addressed Edith and her father aroused my anger, and, entering the room I said ; "Please save your cheap pathos for amateur theatricals and leave this room at once".

The man before me was about six feet and three inches tall, with broad shoulders and two heavy fists. He looked down upon me with an ironical glance and said : "I will spare you this time, old man, but the next occasion that you indulge in impudent language, I will put you in a bag and dump you into Massachusetts Bay".

Before I could answer this pleasing threat, Mr. Fest had left the room and the house.

"Who is this man ?" I asked, turning to Dr. Leete, with no attempt to conceal my displeasure.

"He is a machinist, a very able man in his trade
and a captain in the industrial army", explained the
doctor. "His parents lived next door and when he
was a boy, he used to play with Edith".

"If I were to judge the social manners of the officers of the industrial army, by the experience of this
hour, I should have to say that civilization has moved
very slowly and rather backward than ahead", I
remarked.

"It is an extraordinary case of atavism", said Dr.
Leete. "Such hotheadedness is very rare in our
days".

I did not care to begin just now, a conversation
that might have a very unpleasant termination. But I
could not repress the thought that 113 years ago the
manners and morals were such, that lines were drawn
between the two sexes that were invisible but still
recognized by every one having a little sense of propriety, and that a man would hardly have felt as if he
had been encouraged, if it were not the case. I entertained not the slightest doubt that Edith had
behaved as well as any girl of her time. It was the
consequence of the tendency to equalize everything
that had, perhaps, effaced to a certain degree the fine
lines existing 113 years ago between good women and
men. I remembered my question put to Dr. Leete:
"And so the girls of the twentieth century tell their
love"? and the doctor's answer: "If they choose.
There is no more pretense of a concealment of feel-

ing on their part than on the part of their lovers".*)
—Yes, if girls tell their love just as men do, then the
fine lines between the two sexes must be obliterated,
and a feeling of repulsion and uneasiness took poses-
sion of me.

"It may become necessary to place Mr. Fest, at
least for a few months, under medical treatment",
remarked Dr. Leete thoughtfully. "He is certainly in
a high state of excitement, and it is not unlikely that
he may commit a rash act which he would repent
afterwards".

"One hundred and thirteen years ago we would have
placed such a man under bonds to keep the peace,"
I said, considering with terror the idea, that a man
could be placed in an insane asylum for uttering a
few rash words.

"And if, in violation of his bond, he committed a
breach of the peace", said the doctor, "what did you
then do with such a man"?

"We punished him according to the laws covering
the case, either by imprisonment or by a fine, or in
cases of murder, by putting the criminals to death".

"We place a man in whom atavism makes its appearance, in a hospital where competent physicians
take care of him until they consider him sufficiently
cured to be released", said Dr. Leete, with an expression of great satisfaction and kindness, as he
lighted a fresh havana cigar.

"I think you are running no great risk, papa, if you
allow that man to attend to the duties of his posi-

*) Page 266.

tion", Edith remarked. "He is quick tempered and hot-headed ; but he will soon become composed"

"I am not so sure about that", Dr. Leete said slowly. "I remember that he has always shown deep strong feelings whenever he had set his heart upon anything. He may, and he may not, calm down. It is dangerous to take any chances with such a man".

Conflicting sentiments and ideas filled my heart and head. I felt that if I continued the conversation it might end in a conflict with Dr. Leete, and I was in no mood to engage in any discussion with him. So I excused myself on the plea of a bad head ache, and left the house to take a walk.

The experience of the last hour did not savor much of the millennium. Here was a man holding the rank of an officer of the industrial army, and roughly and rudely accusing Edith of flirtation. His behavior certainly did not correspond with the high praise Dr. Leete gave to the culture and education of the young people of the twentieth century. At all events this conflict between Fest and the family of Dr. Leete demonstrated that contentment is not secured to humanity by the simple introduction of communism, by securing for everybody lodging, clothing and a sufficient quantity of good food. Envy and jealousy threatened our love, and Mr. Fest seemed to be just the kind of a man to make his displeasure felt. The manner in which Dr. Leete proposed to prevent a rash act of the enraged lover appeared to me even more disagreeable than the prospect of a personal encounter with Mr. Fest. And again the question arose before my mind whether Edith Bartlett, my fiancée of 1887 would ever have given a man an opportunity to accuse her of flirtation or to assert that she had encouraged him to declare his love.

When I met Mr. Forest after my next lecture I remarked: "I understand the girls of the twentieth century are somewhat of the style that we would have called emancipated".

With a short but sharp glance at my pale face which testified that I had passed a sleepless night, Mr. Forest replied: "The mad endeavor to equalize the variety, established by nature, has not spared the relations between women and men. Both sexes belong to the industrial army, both have their own officers and judges, both receive the same pay. The queen of your old-fashioned household has been dethroned. We take our meals in great steam-feeding establishments, and if our Radicals, who are in fact the logical communists, are victorious, we will all live together in lodging houses accommodating thousands of people. Marriage will be abolished, together with religion and all personal property; free love will be proclaimed and we will live together like a flock of rabbits. The natural sense of propriety which is a distinguishing quality of the finer sex, fortunately prevents most of our women and girls becoming victims of the low and degrading theories of communism. But the real girl of our period is a very remarkable although by no means agreeable specimen. Do you know Miss Cora Delong, a cousin of Miss Edith Leete"?

"I have not the pleasure"

"You will not escape her", Mr. Forest predicted with a smile of amusement. "Miss Cora is very enthusiastic over the absolute equality of women and men. And since some of our young men are courting their young lady friends, Miss Cora thinks it but fair and proper that she should court some of the young men. She does not hesitate to tell them that she admires their good looks, that she loves them; she asks them for kisses, invites them to a drink—just as young men talk to young girls and just as they invite them to have a plate of ice cream.—She smokes cigars and plays billiards with her male friends, and is doing all she can to "equalize" the sexes. And Miss Cora as well as the other "girls of our period" complains very loudly that she cannot abolish all the differences between woman and man".

"I am not very anxious to make the acquaintance of Miss Cora Delong", I confessed. "And I agree with you from my own personal experience that the old style of housekeeping is very agreeable. I would prefer it. But do not the women of the twentieth century lead a more comfortable life than even the wealthy ladies of my former days? And are you not getting more toil out of the women than we did? Dr. Leete says you are"*).

"Dr. Leete is a great optimist whenever communism is discussed", answered Mr. Forest. "It is, of course,

*) Page 266.

impossible to state with any degree of certainty, how much the girls and women of the year 1887 produced. But I doubt very much the statement of your host that we are getting a great deal more toil out of our women than you did".

"The separate cooking, washing and ironing at the end of the nineteenth century must have caused a great deal more work than the present way of doing these things", I remarked. "And Dr. Leete said : There is no housework to be done"*).

"This is one of the many wild statements of Dr. Leete", Mr. Forest answered. "Who is sweeping the rooms, making the beds, cleaning the windows, dusting the furniture, scrubbing the floors? I have no doubt that Dr. Leete's family is an exception, because women of the industrial army do a great deal, if not all, this work in the house of the leader of the administration party. Have you ever seen Mrs. Leete or Miss Edith doing any housework of the kind I have mentioned"?

I had to confess that I never had, and, indeed, Miss Edith had never done anything except arrange a bunch of flowers. If she were a member of the industrial army, it must be in a capacity, where there was but very little work to do. She had never mentioned that she had duties to perform, and I remembered that Dr. Leete had once spoken of his daughter as an indefatigable shopper**), thus indicating that she had much spare time.

*) Page 118.
**) Page 99.

"In the houses occupied by the rank and file of our industrial army the women have no help from other members of the auxiliary corps (the women of the industrial army). These women have to do all the work I have mentioned, and for them the cooking in the public eating houses is not such a great help as Dr. Leete seems to believe", began Mr. Forest. "These women have to change their dresses three times a day, for they cannot appear at the table in the wrapper they wear while working at home, and they have to wash and dress their children, if they have any. And I am inclined to believe that by having the cooking done in the public eating houses, a great deal of material is squandered that would be saved in a private house. Besides, the public cooking houses have to prepare a large bill of fare, and there is, as a matter of course, a great deal left over that can not be used afterwards. — Therefore, the women who are members of the industrial army find actually very little time to do any work besides the labor connected with housekeeping, and the majority of them would rather do the cooking at home. They could do it while busy with their housework, without losing more time than the dressing and undressing for breakfast, dinner and supper consume. And the complaint has frequently been made that families with many children would fare much better, and the mothers of such families save much time if the cooking were done at home. When there is sickness in the family, it is very annoying to the healthy members to be obliged to go to the eating houses to procure proper food for the invalid. A Mrs. Hosmer said to me the other day, she and her seven children had frequently missed a meal, because she could not wash all her little ones and dress herself and the children in time".

"How do you employ the married women"? I asked.

"This is a very weak point in our social system", Mr. Forest replied. "Most of the married women do not at all relish doing outside work, and they make all kinds of excuses to avoid it. Trouble with their children and personal indisposition are frequently used as excuses for the absence of married women from their positions in the industrial army".

"I suppose it is very difficult, even for the physicians, to ascertain whether such statements are well founded or not", I remarked.

"Of course, in the majority of cases it is impossible to make the charge of shamming and prove it", Mr. Forest continued. "It is this trouble with the married women, and their excuses that their small children prevent them doing any duty in the industrial army, that the radical Communists are using in support of their demand for the abolition of private housekeeping. The Radicals claim that their system would be more prosperous than ours. It would be much cheaper to lodge ·hundreds or thousands under one roof, than to have houses for one, two or three families. They furthermore claim that if marriages were

abolished and free love introduced as the principle
governing the relations of the two sexes, the passing
alliances of men and women would produce better
children than the offspring of the present marriages.
These children would be kept and nursed, after they
had passed their first year, in large nurseries, so that
the mothers would have nothing to do with them and
could attend all day to their work as members of the
industrial army".

"How beastly are these theories"! I exclaimed.
"To establish all human institutions, the relations of
the sexes, simply on a basis of calculation, and to
separate the mothers from their children, because it
is cheaper to raise two hundred mammifers by the
bulk even if the mortality should be ten and twenty
percent larger"!

"But the Radicals are the logical Communists",
Mr. Forest said. "The fundamental principle of
communism is equality. You can base the demand
for the equal division of the products of labor on that
principle of equality only, and if we are all equal,
then there is no reason why we should live in houses
of different architecture, why we should wear different
clothing, why we should have a variety of meals, why
one man should not have just as good a right to the
love of a certain girl as any and all other men, and
why one girl should not have just as fair a claim to
the love of any man she may select as any other girl
has. And there is no reason, why one baby should
have more care than another and why one mother

should spend more time on her child than another, thus perhaps losing time that would have enabled her to make herself useful by peeling a plate of potatoes. The Radicals are the only Communists".

"But every girl can not love all the men, and every man can not very well love all the girls", I objected, somewhat amused by the grim humor displayed by Mr. Forest, although my deep disgust for the abominable brutality preached by the Radicals, prevented real merriment.

"Our radical reformers have never been able to explain to my entire satisfaction how the principle of free love should be regulated, if regulated at all", Mr. Forest answered. "Some of them seem disposed to grant permission to live together, so long as both parties like each other. But the more radical and logical communists object to the stability of an institution as incongruous with the spirit of institutions based on the principle of absolute equality. Perhaps they favor the choosing of a new partner every day, and in order to place both sexes on equal footing they would give the right of choice to the women on Mondays, Wednesdays and Fridays, and to the men on the other three week-days, leaving the Sundays in addition to the ladies. And to avoid strife, when a number of reformers demand the love of the same girl, or when more girls than one fall in love with the same man, they could draw lots or could raffle for the first chance, thus doing justice to all"*).

"It is inconceivable", I said, "that men, proudly considering themselves the crown of creation, or if they do not believe in God, at least considering themselves intellectual free-thinkers, can breed in their brains such horrid theories. I should deplore the fate of womanhood if these theories should ever become victorious, if free love in this damnable form should ever be proclaimed; or if the nursing and education of children should be taken away from the mothers and entrusted to others".

"I should consider it the most terrible blow ever aimed at humanity if the nursing and the first education of the young children should be transferred from their mothers to other persons No women or men, however good and noble they may be, can feel the love and the patience for a child that fills a mother's heart. The ties that bind women and men together, marriage and the family, are institutions which even our communistic Solons have so far respected. Humanity is doomed to barbarism on the day family life is broken up, when mothers are separated from their

*) The well known naturalist, Professor Karl Vogt in Germany, famous by his nickname "Monkey-Vogt," is a radical philosopher, who gained this sobriquet as an advocate of the theory of evolution, claiming Monkeys to have the same progenitors as man. But even Vogt's radicalism revolted against the doctrines set forth by Russian, French and German nihilists and anarchists; during a "convention" held in Switzerland, Karl Vogt dedicated the following lines to them:

"Wir wollen in der Sonn' spazieren,
Wir wollen uns mit Fett beschmieren

children, when men are alienated from the constantly elevating influence of good women, when the relations of men and women are stripped of that sublimity conferred upon matrimonial life by the permanent exchange of feelings and thoughts, when these relations are degraded to nothing but sexual intercourse. Nearly all our good qualities can be traced back to the influence the unfathomable love and patience of the mother, in her efforts to make her beloved child good and true, have exercised upon our minds and hearts. Nearly all great men had good mothers. There is nothing on earth that could compensate a child for the loss of its mother, or that could indemnify humanity for the loss of the beneficial influence mothers have on the growing generation".

"Do you suppose that your Radicals will ever have power enough to dethrone the mothers and to abolish matrimonial life"? I asked, with great curiosity.

Mr. Forest's reply to this question sounded very cheerful and confident, more so than anything he had thus far uttered in my presence.

Und ausgelöscht sei Mein und Dein.
Wir wollen uns mit Schnapps berauschen,
Wir wollen uns're Weiber tauschen,
Wir wollen freie Männer sein!''

A free translation of which reads:

We will walk in the sun, boys, with ease,
We will cover our bodies with grease,
For poverty there is no need.
We'll all get as drunk as a loon,
We'll swap our wives every noon,
And thus be *true* freemen indeed.

"The Radicals may rise and overthrow the present government, they may change many things", he said, "and they may not meet with much resistance, because the great mass of the people simply tolerate the present rule, have no love for it, and will not rally to its defense. But the experience of our Radicals will be very unpleasant if they attempt to separate man and wife, mother and child. Almost every mother will fight like a lioness before she will give up her children, and I know one man who does not care a straw for the overthrow of the present government, but who would fight to his death before he would yield to a separation from his spouse. For a good and loving wife always has been, is, and always will be the greatest blessing of God, and no man of honor and courage will permit anybody to rob him of her"!

CHAPTER VI.

"Now, Mr. Forest", I said when I again met my predecessor as professor of the history of the nineteenth century, "please tell me how much is the average yearly income of every inhabitant of the United States of America"?

"The average yearly income was figured up to be $204.", Mr. Forest answered.

"Two hundred and four dollars you say. Is that all"? I queried with astonishment. "I expected from the statements of Dr. Leete and his style of living that it amounted to at least three times that sum".

Forest smiled. "How much was the average income of the people of the United States in your days"? he asked.

I was forced to admit that I had not the faintest idea.

"It was $165.", said Mr. Forest, "or about twice the average amount earned by the people of Germany or France".

I was perplexed. I had never looked into the statistics of national economy. I had spent about twenty times $165. every year. I remembered having read in the papers of my time that the average yearly earnings of the working men, working women and children were over four hundred dollars, and I was inclined to estimate the average yearly income at about six hundred dollars. I stated this to Mr. Forest.

"You have left out of your calculation the women and children who were not earning anything, but who depended upon the income of their husbands, fathers and brothers", Mr. Forest explained. "An income of two hundred and four dollars for every man, woman and child would, therefore, represent a large increase, if the figures were fairly given. But they are not correct. In order to make the income of the nation appear greater than it really is, the value of the various productions is quoted higher than in your days. Consequently the purchasing power of every dollar on our credit-cards is less than that of the dollar of your time. I have carefully compared the prices of all the necessities and commodities as they are now and as they were in your time, and I have found an increase of about 95 percent. The real average yearly income of all the people of our country is about one hundred and twelve dollars, so there is not an increase of about 24 percent, but a decrease of about 33 percent".

"How do you account for this remarkable statement"? I inquired.

"That is a question easier asked than answered", replied Mr. Forest.

"I am very curious to hear your explanation", I remarked. "Dr. Leete has given me so many plausible reasons for the "poverty resulting from our extraordinary industrial system"†) that I was quite convinced of the greater wealth of your people. He mentioned the frequent wrong speculations of the nineteenth century, the insane competition, the periodical overproductions and consequent crises, the waste from idle capital and labor*), and he especially dwelt upon the point that four or five enterprises of the nineteenth century failed where one succeeded"**).

"Yes, I know Dr. Leete's arguments from occasional speeches he has made, and from articles he has written for the administration organs", Mr. Forest responded. "And he has undoubtedly mentioned many other causes that crippled the production of your days. He has, or he may have, pointed to the expenditures for your army and navy, to your custom and revenue officials, to the tax-assessors and collectors you employed, to the larger number of judges, sheriffs and other officers you needed, to the greater amount of labor made necessary by domestic washing and cooking, to the large number of middlemen needed in handling goods before the articles made their way from the factory to the retail store, the latter corresponding to our storehouses. And Dr. Leete has or may have, mentioned the lawyers, bankers and their clerks who were nominally engaged in

†) Page 42.
*) Page 229 & 230.
**) Page 230.

work that was really not done, and which has all been done away with to-day".

"Indeed", I said, "Dr. Leete has enumerated most of these causes of the poverty of our days, and, since these evils have been abolished under your system of production, I think it would be simply a matter of course that the total yearly income of your people should have increased, and I wonder that the increase is not even greater than you have stated it to be".

"I will not waste much time in investigating all these points and ascertaining how great was the loss thus inflicted on the production of the nineteenth century", Mr. Forest continued. "But you seem to be inclined to overestimate their effects. Unlucky speculations, for instance, caused sometimes heavy losses to the speculator, but in most cases they produced values that benefitted others and increased the wealth of the nation. The "insane competition" made goods cheaper, thereby stimulating both production and consumption and not harming, but on the contrary to a certain extent benefitting humanity. The statement that four or five enterprises failed where one succeeded is a "licentia poetica" of which Dr. Leete makes free use. You must know yourself that it is a gross exaggeration.

The saving from the employment of steam-cooking we have already investigated. If there is any, it is small in the cities and smaller still in the country districts, and offers no compensation for the loss of comfort involved. Furthermore we take into consideration that many of the men engaged as judges, lawyers, bankers, officers, middlemen, or clerks were over forty-five years or under twenty-one, so that you would have to deduct them from the force that you have to consider as a loss to the industrial army".

"Still, these misplacements of capital and labor, these losses in various ways were enormous", I insisted, "and they account for the greater poverty of the people of the nineteenth century, compared with the inhabitants of the United States in the year 2000".

"They would, undoubtedly", Mr. Forest argued, "if there were no other reasons for a *decrease* of our production. But there are causes as you will readily see, when I point them out. The principle reason why both the quantity and the quality of our production are constantly abating, is the *abolishment of competition.* Competition was the gigantic motor that caused nearly everybody during the first nineteen centuries of Christian civilization to use all his mental and physical powers to "get ahead". Since the introduction of communism, since the good workmen are robbed of a part of the products of their labor for the benefit of the poor workers, and since everybody is sure of an equal share of all the necessities and commodities of life, no matter how much or how little he produces, the masses of the people are becoming more and more indifferent. They are not putting forth their best efforts to furnish much and good work. They are taking life easy. Their mental and physical ability has decreased. The people of the United States, once famous for their energy, are degenerating Promotion might have acted as a spur, had not favoritism of the politicians monopolized all good positions for the tools of the administration".

"The second reason for the decrease of production is the shortening of both the years and the hours of work. It is difficult to ascertain how many persons of different ages were employed in your time in productive labor. The census of the United States government taken before you went to sleep for one hundred and thirteen years, the census of 1880 is in many respects a very creditable work but it does not give the ages of the persons who then formed the industrial army. The report is very elaborate as to the number of persons of all ages, their nationality, and so forth. But in regard to the age of the workers it only gives three classes, one comprising all the persons under 15 years of age, another, all persons between 16 and 59, and the third, the number of employees of 60 years and over. Of the people under 15 years of age 1,118,356 were employed, of the men and women over 60 years 933,644 were males and 70,873 females. The whole industrial army of your day numbered, out of an entire population of 50,155,-783, not less than 17,392,099, only 2,647,157 being girls and women, including the servant girls".

"I remember reading some of these figures", I remarked.

"The census of 1880 thus shows that over 12 percent of the population of the United States belonging to the industrial army were under 15 and over 60 years of age", Mr. Forest continued. "This is, of course, a very bad showing. Girls and boys under 15 years of age should certainly belong to the schools, while people over 50 years ought to have permanent rest and a good living. But there can be no doubt that the working-force at the close of the last century was comparatively larger than ours. According to the census of 1880, there lived in the United States 15,527,215 persons of the age, that would make them to-day members of our industrial army. You em - ployed, therefore, 2,173,184 more persons than your whole population between the ages of 21 to 45 num- bered, and this calculation figures, that all the people of that age are really active. You must consider the fact, that many of our population who are of the age, when they ought to do work in the industrial army, are excused from service for various reasons, for in - stance: permanently sick people, the weak-minded, cripples, mothers of babies, etc. You must, therefore, recognize that your people furnished a much stronger working-force than does our generation."

"I guess we did", I admitted, convinced by the figures quoted by Mr. Forest.

Drawing a piece of paper from his note book the gentleman continued: "Here is a list of all the avoca- tions you may call unproductive, taken from the census of 1880. I have given every point, which seems contrary to my views, the benefit of the doubt. I have embraced all the trades, professions and occupations Dr. Leete himself could fairly claim as non-productive in this compilation, though a good many of the people engaged in them were, at least, saving time for members of the producing classes. Many men and women of your time would not have been able to produce pictures and works of art, or to sing in operas and so forth, if it had been impossible for them to secure help in housekeeping. Now, in your day, the year of our Lord 1880, the people engaged in the occupations, trades and professions that Dr. Leete would call nonproductive, numbered 1,654,319 including all the servants. Deducting these 1,654,319 from the 2,173,084 persons under the age of 15 and over 60, there still would be a surplus of 518,765 women and men of your time over the number of people, that would belong in our days to the industrial force"

"Your figures are correct, as far as you state them", I said, desirous to encourage Mr. Forest to proceed with his argument.

"So you had, undoubtedly, in 1880 a surplus of productive persons above the age that would place them in our industrial army, which amounted to over one percent of the population, and to over three percent of persons at the age where they, to-day, would have to be members of the industrial army, even if we deduct all the persons from the working force whom a man like Dr. Leete would classify as non-productive Now, deduct, furthermore, all our ladies occupied by their duties as mothers, before and after the birth of their children, deduct all the persons permanently sick, all the cripples and all the other people unable to do productive work, and you will have to admit that you had in your days a comparatively much larger force engaged in productive labor than we have. Consider, that these people were stimulated by competition, that they desired to establish themselves on an independent basis, that they put forth their best efforts, in order to secure a life free from care during their old age, and that, therefore, the years of productive labor of each individual were much longer than they are at present, and that the stimulus to succeed was a potent fact in obtaining more and better work than we can secure nowadays.

"That I will admit", I answered.

"And the working hours to-day are much shorter than they were at the end of the nineteenth century", proceeded Mr. Forest with an expression on his face like that of a victor in a gladiatorial fight. "The natural tendency of an organization of society like ours is in that direction. And there are many reasons to encourage such a tendency. I have mentioned already that the farmers are complaining of the small number of theaters and concert halls and other amusements and advantages for country people, which city people enjoy to the full. The consequence of this is, that the country people flock to the cities. The nation would have suffered from a want of agricultural products if all the people crowding into the large cities had been accepted. But they were not welcomed.

They were appointed to farm work. That settled
their desire to live in the cities, and at the same time
destroyed their ambition. The country people are satisfied that they cannot improve their lot, that they
have to do farm work and that the city people are im-
posing upon them. The consequence is that they
are working as little as possible, and the farming products have decreased to such an extent that we have to
appoint city workmen of class B of the third grade to
farm work, in order to protect the city people from
starvation",

"Say your worst", I remarked with a forced smile,
for I saw Dr. Leete's beautiful structure crumbling
under the fire of Mr. Forest's artillery of logic. .

"You have seen", Mr. Forest continued, "that the
industrial army of 1880, engaged in productive labor,
was, in proportion, much larger than ours, that the
members were stimulated by competition to use their
best mental and physical efforts to 'get ahead', and
that they worked longer hours than we do. You must,
furthermore, consider that we squander a greater
amount of labor in overseeing and bookkeeping than
you ever did. Most of your retail business was trans-
acted on the cash basis, and the small tradespeople
did their own bookkeeping after closing their stores
and shops. We, on the other hand, have an account
for every man, woman and child in the country in the
books of the national administration*). We have a
bureau which keeps an account of the visits of all the

*) Page 87.

physicians*). We have another bureau where you can secure help for housework as well as for other purposes, where accounts are kept, both of the helpers and of the people who demand help.**) We have bureaus for each industry and they are excellent examples of the most thorough manner in which a government can waste human labor. The entire field of productive and constructive industry is, as you know, divided into ten great departments, each representing a group of allied industries, each particular industry being in turn represented by a subordinate bureau, which has a complete record of the plant and force under its control, as well as of the present product and the means of increasing it. The estimates of consumption of the distribution department (an organization independent ot the great productive departments) after adoption by the administration, are sent as mandates to the ten great departments which allot them to the subordinate bureaus representing the particular industries, and these set the men to work. Each bureau is responsible for the task given it, and the responsibility is enforced by departmental supervision and that of the administration; nor does the distribution department accept the products without its own inspection, while, even if in the hands of the consumer, an article turns out unfit, the system enables the fault to be traced back to the original workman".†)

*) Page 122.
**) Page 120.
†) Pages 182, 183.

"This amount of overseeing and bookkeeping, by which the government can trace back to the original workman a bad pin or a poorly rolled cigar, enables the administration to provide for its favorites many desirable places, but it certainly lessens the productive power of the industrial force, thus, again, decreasing the production. And at the same time the number of consumers is larger than in your days".

"How do you account for this?" I inquired.

"Has not Dr. Leete informed you that persons of average constitution usually live to be from eighty-five to ninety years old?"*)

"Indeed, he has".

"This accounts for an increased number of consumers who all draw their full share of the products of labor in the form of a credit card", Mr. Forest continued. "Our people live longer than your contemporaries did. They take life easy, and while the spirit, the energy and the enterprise of our generation are gradually decreasing and degenerating, their bodies last longer".

"Ah! now at last you are admitting one gain", I exclaimed.

"If it is a gain, I do", rejoined Mr. Forest. "But even the favored members of our industrial army do not seem to consider it a very valuable acquisition. Because the only way to secure a desirable position is to sacrifice their own independence and that of their relatives and friends, and even to employ base means

*) Page 197.

of corruption, downright bribery of their superiors
with a part of their own credit cards, many of the
favorites of the administration are, in fact, enemies of
the leaders".

After a short pause Mr. Forest concluded his arguments. "I suppose I have successfully demonstrated
that our organization of society, with its pretended
basis of human equality has proved to be a failure,
that there prevails to-day an inequality in many respects more oppressive than that of your time, that
favoritism and corruption are about as potent under
our communistic rule as they were at the end of the
nineteenth century, that personal liberty is almost entirely destroyed, that the members of the industrial
army, without having the right to vote at the election
of their superiors, are at the mercy of their officers,
that the members of the industrial force who are considered enemies of the government are leading a life
that very properly may be styled as twenty-four years
of hell on earth, that since the abolishment of competition the people are mentally degenerating for want
of intellectual exercise, and that not even a greater
wealth is a consolation for the loss of the greater liberty and independence the people enjoyed in your
time. The shortening of both the years and the hours
of productive labor, the abolition of competition and
the increase in the number of consumers have reduced
the average daily income of the inhabitants of the
United States to such an extent that the amount in-
scribed upon our credit card is so small, that it af-

fords only a very frugal living to the people of the twentieth century.   And there is no doubt in my mind that a continuation of the present system for a few hundred years more would so degrade and degenerate the people that a relapse into barbarism would ensue"

CHAPTER VII.

'You have given me your ideas and objections in regard to the present state of affairs", I commenced my next conversation with Mr. Forest, "you have expressed, occasionally, your conviction that the organization of society at the end of the last century needed reformation. Will you, now, kindly state how you would have reformed the evils of my time?"

Mr. Forest smiled. "I do not pretend to be a reformer who can perfect mankind or even all human institutions. Please do not forget that we are all cooking with water. What many people style the social question is insolvable. The variety established by nature will always be felt. You can never create conformity. We will always have smart and stupid, industrious and lazy people. The clever women and men will not submit to an equal distribution of the product of labor, nor feel satisfied under such a state of legal robbery. And if the results of labor are distributed according to the ability of the workers the people earning less than others will always grumble. It is, therefore, impossible to make all men content with their lot, no matter how you may distribute the earnings of the working force. But the fact that it is impossible to make everybody absolutely happy does not release us from the obligation to use our best efforts toward improving the lot of mankind".

"I understand your position. But let me hear what reforms you would have inaugurated or proposed, if you had lived at the close of the last century".

"The society of your day suffered chiefly", said Mr. Forest, "from unsystematized production, the monopolies that made possible the amassing of immense fortunes at the expense of the people, and the want of intelligence on the part of the workers who would either submit to these extortions or strike, instead of forming mutual producing associations. Another great evil was the injustice of your taxation. In all the fields of human activity the workers produced values without a clear knowledge of what was really required. There was, generally, such a surplus of the products of farming that the farmers had to sell everything so cheap that they could hardly earn a living. Some factories worked day and night until the markets were overstocked with goods. Then these goods were sold at any price obtainable, sometimes below cost. Numerous bankruptcies followed, the factories had to, stop their work, and the manufacturers as well as the working women and men had to suffer from a term of idleness until the surplus of goods was exhausted. Then a feverish activity commenced again".

"How would you have remedied this evil?" I asked.

"A national bureau of statistics should have ascertained both the average yearly consumption and the capacity of the different trades and their plants for the production of the necessities of life".

"Should the government have given to each trade an order for the work to be done during the year?" I queried, "and how should the trades have divided such an order among the members so that all would be satisfied?"

"The National Government should simply have ascertained the amount of the yearly consumption of the various articles, the capacity of the respective trades for furnishing such articles, and should then have left the regulation of production to the members of each trade. Such an arrangement would have given each trade a clear idea of its task. The chosen representatives of each trade could have subdivided the work. A heavy overproduction would easily have been prevented, while competition both among the factories and the individual members would have been maintained, thus securing the best kind of work, while under the present system of production we are suffering from a want both of quantity and quality".

"But if any trade should have produced more goods than needed", I objected.

"That would have been its own fault, and it would, as a matter of course, have had to stand the consequences", Mr. Forest replied.

"But, suppose, the members of a certain trade had formed a trust, thereby forcing the people to pay exorbitant prices for the products of their guilds?" I objected again.

"A national law should have protected the people against an attempted robbery of this kind, threatening all guilty parties with confiscation of all their property and with the operation of all the plants by men hired by the administration, until the plants could be sold to operators. The importation of the respective goods from other countries would cover the deficiency until all the plants were again in full operation".

"But how would you have stopped the frequent strikes of our days?" I asked.

"By encouraging the workman to start mutual producing associations", Mr. Forest answered. "I have mentioned already how mutual producing associations could easily have been started. A dozen tailors or shoemakers could have rented lofts with steam power, purchased a few sewing and other machines and sold their products directly to other workmen, thus securing the profits of tne manufacturer, wholesaler, retailer and workman, or in other words all the profit that was in the labor of the members of the association. There was no law in your time to forbid such enterprises or to prevent all other workmen from buying their boots, shoes, clothing, furniture and al other articles from such associations solely. As soon as the manufacturers noticed that all the laborers were commencing to deal with mutual associations they would gladly have sold their plants at a very fair price, and yet cheaper than a new association could have procured them. I imagine there was very little pleasure in conducting a factory or any other business having many employees in 1887, judging from the frequent strikes that made it almost impossible for many business men to figure on prices six months ahead, or to close contracts. Therefore, the owners of factories would, I fancy, have sold their plants at very fair prices. And the workmen could not have done a smarter thing than to cause the former manufacturers to remain with them as business managers at a fair salary. This would have secured a smooth running of the concern. Under such an arrangement the workers would have become the owners of the business concerns, paying for them in installments, they would have secured full pay for their work, and the former owner would have disposed of all his former cares, receiving a fair compensation for his plant and his services".

"I think that most of the manufacturers and businessmen of my days were so worried by the constantly increased demands of their employees, that they would have gladly sold their property", I remarked, "but what would have become of the wholesale and retail dealers?"

"They could have sold their goods and have either joined the producing associations as salesmen or gone into another business", Mr. Forest replied. "And in a similar way the workmen of your time could have organized one trade after another, until the entire manufacturing industry had been based on large guilds, the latter consisting mostly of mutual producing societies".

"But our workmen preferred to avoid the responsibility, care and risk of business enterprises. They would rather have worked for wages and, occasionally tried to increase them, sometimes by striking and preventing other laborers taking the places of the strikers", I said. "You are aware of this state of affairs?"

"Yes", Forest answered, "and it must have been a sad spectacle to see intelligent men who could just as well have been independent, remain journeymen, trying to bulldoze their employer to pay them more than he volunteered, and to intimidate other workers from performing duties at a rate of wages that would have satisfied them. The fact that your workingmen did not possess sufficient enterprise, mental discipline and independence, to establish mutual producing associations, has driven humanity into communism. That this damnable form of society is a failure is a matter of course. When humanity was at so low a standard that shoemakers had not spunk or smartness enough to start and run the shoeshops on a co-operative basis, and tailors could not manage tailorshops on a similar plan, it was simply impossible to make successful an organization which had the power to regulate all production and all consumption. But the principle of mutual productive associations is, in my opinion, the one best adapted for the solution of the labor question, because it secures for the members of the associations the pay for the full real value of their labor and keeps alive competition, tne strongest factor in securing the progress of mankind. But whether we shall ever reach this solution of the labor question seems doubtful".

"I am inclined to believe in your plan", I admitted, "so far as laborers engaged in manufacturing establish ments are concerned. But how would you have organized the work on the farms, the employment of professional man, railroad officials and laborers, employees on streetcars, merchants and bankers and their clerks and those who follow many other avocations?"

"Let us go slowly", Mr. Forest answered with a smile. "Let us first look into the agrarian question. Reformers of society have always met the greatest difficulty when they came across the farmers. Under communistic rule the country people have but very little love for the soil they are tilling because they know it is not theirs, that their toiling does not benefit them, and they feel that the city people are favored at their expense. If I had been asked at the end of the last century how I would treat the land question I would have advocated a law ordaining that no farmer should have more than forty acres of land. If any farmer had more at the time of the passing of the bill he could keep it during his lifetime, but he would be compelled to dispose of it in his last will, so that a single person should not receive more than forty acres. On a forty acre piece a farmer can make a fair living, and although the farmers were by no means prosperous in your days, yet there was still a fair prospect for the increase of the value of land by reason of the increase of the population, augmented as it was by immigration".

"But how would you have proposed to stop over-production by the farming population through which the agricultural interests were suffering in 1887?" I inquired.

"Fhe National Bureau of Statistics would have served the farmers just as well as the rest of the people. The farmers should have formed state associations and should have lald out plans for the production according to the capacity of the farms. And, after ascertaining that their capacity of production was far ahead of consumption, they should have used the surplus of land for the productton of new things that could, perhaps, find a market, or they could have saved their labor by not producing more goods than they could sell in supplying the real demands of the market, thus working less."

"Under your plan every person would not have had a right to land", I remarked.

"Yes, everybody would, who could pay the price the owner demanded for it", Mr. Forest said. "Not everybody can own a farm. Did you own one?"

"I did not".

"Very well. Under your communistic system nobody owns a piece of ground large enough to put a stick into".

"How would you have regulated the professional services?"

"By passing laws establishing rates to be charged for professional services. And the laws I would have simplified by doing away with the abominable confusion resulting from the innumerable decisions forming precedents. For a long time I did not believe it until I found positive statements to the effect that a trading nation like the Americans, at the end of the nineteenth century, had neither a national criminal law, nor a national commerce law. This fact and the confusion caused by the conflicting precedent decisions that could always be quoted by either of the contesting lawyers in a suit must have made the United States, in your days, a paradise for swindlers and for lawyers who cared not so much for the upholding of the law, as for a retainer".

"Such were the charges frequently made against the law and lawyers in my days", I said. "But now tell me what you would have done with the railroad and telegraph employees, with—"

"Let us stop right here", Mr. Forest interrupted. "I would have purchased all the railroads and all the telegraph lines of the country at a fair price. I would have issued United States bonds to pay for them. I would have used the income of the roads and lines to pay running expenses and the interest on the bonds issued, and the surplus in the United States treasury I would have applied to paying off the bonds".

"But would not this proposition of yours, if carried into effect, have brought about the same horrors you declare the concentration of power in the hands

of the administration has brought down on humanity
of the twentieth century?" I asked.

"No. For that the officers would not be numerous
enough", Mr. Forest replied; "and I remember distinctly, that in your days civil service reform had
been instituted, to a certain extent, in the appointment
of federal officers. I have read conflicting opinions
about it. Some writers claimed a frequent change of
the officers to be a fundamental principle of republican
institutions. Others ridiculed this notion. Every
man of common sense would keep a man who knew
and performed the duties of his position well. And
the nation should simply do the same regardless of
the party affiliations of the employee, thus securing a
good public service. I remember that letter carriers
and other employees of the postoffice department
could not be removed without cause. Now, if this
principle had been applied to all the clerical and subordinate officers, if all the railroad and telegraph officials, when the nation took charge of these institutions,
had been retained at the salaries they were receiving at
that time, so long as they did their work well, then
there would have been no trouble. Uncle Sam would
have paid just as much, if not more, than the former
corporations did, and by retaining the whole force he
could have united the railroad and telegraph lines
with the postal service after the fashion already prevailing, at that time, in Germany".

"That theory sounds very plausible, certainly".

"It is very remarkable that such a smart and ener-
getic people, *trading* as much as our forefathers did,

should have allowed the principal means of commerce, the railroad and telegraph lines, to be in the hands of private corporations which, as a matter of course, managed them simply with a view of paying as large dividends as possible to the shareholders,—sometimes for "a wheel within a wheel", for members of the inner circle. In the historical works of your time I frequently note expressions of astonishment and wrath because knights, during the fourteenth and fifteenth centuries in Europe, stopped merchants passing the roads below their castles, and demanded a part of the travellers' goods as a toll, or the payment of a certain sum of money for which they agreed either to let the merchants travel in peace or to furnish them with protection for the rest of their journey. These knights had to risk their lives when they undertook to collect a toll from the merchants, for the latter not unfrequently showed fight; they knew how to handle a lance or a sword and they had their goods protected by armed men. More than one of the enterprising, toll-levying knights died on the highway, where he had tried to attach a share of the merchant's earnings. But the gentlemen controlling the highways of traffic at the end of the last century could levy new tolls, whenever they pleased. All they had to do was to sit down in Delmonico's or some other good restaurant, and over a few bottles of champagne resolve to do so. There was no danger connected with this business of toll levying in your days, Mr. West, except the danger of a headache when the champagne happened to be poor. It was a very remarkable state of affairs, and it is a striking proof of the general fairness and good nature of the railroad magnates of 1887 that they treated the people as well as they did. Still, it was a ridiculous spectacle to see the principal highways of such a business people controlled by private corporations that virtually did precisely what they pleased".

"The gas works, street railways and waterworks of cities you would have had managed by the city authorities, I suppose?" I said.

"Indeed, that is what I would have done", Mr. Forest replied. "But I would first have extended the power of the national administration over all the forest and mining lands then in the possession of the United States. If the national government had taken care of the remnants of the immense forests that once covered the larger part of this vast territory, we would not at present suffer from a lack of timber".

"What would you have done with the bankers and merchants?"

"Nothing", Mr. Forest answered. "The different mutual productive associations would have needed men to manage such business affairs as were outside the management of the factory, attended to by the former manufacturer. For the workmen would soon have found out that it required more than the manual labor of the toilers to build up and run a large business establishment. And the owners of grocery stores would, if similar establishments had been started by consuming societies, have sold their stock on hand

and secured places as managers or clerks of the new stores".

"I suppose that under the system proposed by you all the old-fashioned stores would have been forced to close out", I said, "because the different guilds would have purchased goods at wholesale and would have sold them to their members at a low cash price. The storekeepers that were not able to secure positions in the stores of the different guilds would have been forced to look out for some other employment; —a rather hard lot for many of them".

"The change in the mode of production would not have been sudden", Mr. Forest explained, "but would have been brought about gradually, thus giving the business people, perhaps thirty years time to let their children join guilds instead of becoming storekeepers and traders: And there is no reason why enterprising merchants who had a fine taste in selecting goods, should not have retained a large number of customers. It is not cheapness alone that attracts buyers, and in the country, where there were no factories, etc., close at hand, stores would have to be kept".

"You said you would have passed laws preventing farmers owning more than forty acres of land", I said, "Would you have also limited the amount of city property to be owned by any one man?"

"The possession of one house ought to have satisfied every fair-minded man", Mr. Forest continued. "Nobody can deny that the accumulation of fortunes amounting to many millions in the hands of a few people, while hundreds of thousands could earn hardly more than a living, was a state of affairs which made this damnable communism possible".

"But how would you have been able to prevent this?" I queried with some curiosity.

"By making the taxation of inherited property the principal assessment for the maintenance of the national, state and local governments as well as of the schools. I would have proposed a tax of one percent on all property inherited by a single person, amounting upward to $10,000. An inheritance amounting to $20,000 I would have taxed two percent, $30,000 three percent, $100,000 ten percent, $200,000 twenty percent, $500,000 fifty percent. If anybody left a fortune yielding a larger sum than $250,000 to each heir, the surplus should have been considered as an income to humanity, the national, state and local governments sharing therein in a just proportion".

"Would not such a law have acted as a check upon the ambition and the enterprise of the people?" I asked.

"If it had prevented people amassing immense fortunes it would have served a good purpose. It would not have lessened but protected competition". Mr. Forest answered. "Men possessing twenty or fifty millions of dollars and using them without regard for the rights of other people, were very dangerous. They were in a position to annihilate their competitors, and they frequently used their power unmercifully. Thus by increasing their millions and by killing competition they were paving the way for communism. And was it not unfair that a man who had amassed by all manner of means such an enormous fortune could leave it to a son who would continue the work of killing competitors with smaller means? What could the most able man accomplish in an avocation, if he had against him a man who possessed, perhaps, very little ability, but who was unscrupulously using his millions to attain his ends? Parents might leave their children enough to place their dear ones beyond the reach of want but they should not enable them to prevent the children of poorer parents having a fair show to get ahead in life".

"You would have met with considerable resistance to such a proposition in my days", I remarked.

"I fancy the millionaires would have objected", Mr. Forest assented. "Still, I think that such a law would have served the best interest of both the children of rich parents and humanity in general. Nothing but a law of this kind could have stemmed the tide of communism and anarchy. A child inheriting $250,000 ought to be satisfied with his lot and ought to let the surplus go to the defraying of the expenses of the government. By sacrificing a part of their enormous fortunes, the heirs would have saved the rest, and would have weakened the communistic tendency of your days. And it appears more than doubtful to me whether the possession of such enormous properties made these wealthy people good, or even happy and contented".

"If such a law had been passed in 1887 most of the millionaires would have converted their property into cash and emigrated to Europe", I objected.

"I suppose they would have done so", Mr. Forest admitted. "But I am, nevertheless, convinced that a law of this kind would not only have been just but that it would have done a great deal to save humanity from communism. Civilized countries would have been obliged to pass a similar law at the same time".

"The temptation to avoid the consequences of the statute would have been very great", I remarked. "Many people would have tried to evade the tax by declaring to the authorities a smaller amount of property than they really owned, or by presenting during their life time, a part of their fortune to their children".

"Any attempt at fraud should have been punished by a confiscation of all the property", said Mr. Forest. "And as for gifts they could have been taxed at the same rate as inheritances from one percent up to fifty.—But such a law would have been necessary only during the first fifty or sixty years of a new order of things. As soon as mutual producing associations were in general operation, selling their goods directly from the factories to the consumers, and buying all the necessities of life and commodities, as far as possible, at wholesale, and selling them a little above cost price, there would have been little occasion for men to amass millions of dollars. The numoer of middlemen and traders would have largely decreased. Everybody would have been compelled to do work of some kind and would have received a compensation according to both the quantity and quality of his performances".

"But would not cliques like the one you are charging with having control of your government have taken possession of a mutual producing association, thus depriving the clever workers of a part of their earnings and paying the poorer men more for their work than they deserved?" I queried.

"In such a case the good men could have left an association, where they were cheated and joined another partnership. Good laborers are always appreciated wherever competition rules. But the association, thus driving away their ablest members, would soon have been unable to compete with others. Difficulties, therefore, could have been regulated without much trouble".

"You must advocate, as a matter of course mutual insurance companies among the guilds for the protection of the members against accidents, sickness, infirmity and old age, and these mutual insurance companies would, perhaps, have also written life and fire policies?" I suggested.

"That would, indeed, have been a consequence of the whole system that would unite the few advantages of communism with the benefits of competition", Mr. Forest answered.

"Would you have encouraged immigration?" I asked. "At the end of the nineteenth century, many honest, liberal and fair-minded people, whom nobody could fairly class as know-nothings, were of the opinion that the United States had all the foreign elements the country could assimilate, and that the rest of the public lands should be preserved for the children of the people living in the Union, in the year of our Lord 1887. The objection against further immigration was largely due to the actions of the German and Irish dynamiters".

"I can imagine", Mr. Forest answered, "that some of the customs and notions of the numerous immigrants of your time were objectionable to the native Americans, and that the crimes of the anarchists, their crazy revolt against the laws of a country that had offered them hospitality, must naturally have created a deep emotion among the Anglo-Americans. But I think they had, nevertheless, many reasons for encouraging immigration, especially under your form of production. A strict execution of the laws of the country", he continued, after a pause, "against *all* transgressors, native as well as transplanted, would have done the country good and have made all attempts to restrict immigration entirely unnecessary, all the more so, as the really objectionable foreigners could reach the United States via Canada or Mexico if they desired strongly to become inhabitants of the United States."

"These arguments were frequently used in my time," I remarked.

"The comparatively small harm done by immigrants was largely over-balanced by the many advantages the citizens of the United States obtained through the large influx of people from Europe", said Mr. Forest. "The very fact that hundreds of thousands of able-bodied people, whose rearing and education had cost the European countries millions of dollars, landed on American shores was a great gain to the United States. The very presence of these men and women increased the value of the lands or city lots where they settled, *thus enriching the property owners.* Many of the immigrants were well trained laborers and mechanics, others artists and scholars. All these men and women were not familiar with the ways and means of their new country, many of them were unable to speak the English language, and they all had, therefore, to start in the very lowest places of American business life — *thus naturally elevating all the inhabitants of the United States in a more or less degree, to higher positions in life.* Many of these people, coming from all parts of Europe, were ably and well trained, and they became successfull competitors of those, who were here before their arrival. But the constant stream of people from Europe to the United States *was, nevertheless, steadily enriching and elevating the American people,* and all the blows aimed at immigration were, therefore, unwise, and the legislators who proposed such blows remind me of the man who intended to kill the goose that laid the golden eggs".

"It is, of course, impossible to advance social theories to which everybody will agree", Mr. Forest said in conclusion. "I maintain, however, that all such theories should be based on two fundamental principles. They should have as an aim the establishment of a state of society, where everybody should be protected against an undeserved poverty, where the brain-cancer, fear of an undeserved poverty, should be cured; and they should preserve competition, the power that is permanently spurring everybody to use his best efforts to elevate himself and humanity".

CHAPTER VIII.

When I left Mr. Forest after our last conversation I was convinced, partly by his arguments, partly by my own observations, that communism had not established the millennium, as I had first supposed, after the lectures of Dr. Leete; but that it had degraded humanity in every respect.

I felt that I must speak frankly to Dr. Leete about the change in my convictions, resign my position as professor of Shawmut College, and that this would give my life in the society of the twentieth century a new and unpleasant direction.

Dr. Leete had treated me with the utmost kindness, and if I, from the commencement of our relations, had refused to become enthusiastic over communism, my amiable host, I think, would have not only tolerated my views but would have continued his friendship for me, provided I did not join the active opposition to the administration. He might even have consented to my marriage with Edith. But now the circumstances were such, that my change of mind involved the most unpleasant consequences for Dr. Leete. He had recommended me as a man especially qualified above others to become the successor of Mr. Forest as professor of the history of the nineteenth century. I owed my appointment solely to his influence, and there could be no doubt that my apostacy from communism would seriously injure the respect in which Dr. Leete's advice had been held heretofore. My host would feel this keenly. The rather sudden change in my opinions, the consequence of my very limited knowledge of national economy, could have no other effect upon Dr. Leete's family, than to destroy their good opinion of me. They would be forced to believe me a shallow, superficial and ungrateful man, who had changed from an enthusiastic advocate of communism to such a decided opponent of this theory that I would resign a position granted to me through Dr. Leete's efforts, and thus place my kind host in an embarrassing position.

And how would Edith regard my resignation of the professorship? She was attached to her father by a well founded affection and esteem. Would her love for me prove strong enough to overcome the shock my step involved? My blind enthusiasm for the present order of things had been heralded all over the country by the administration organs; they had pointed to the fact that I, a living witness of the civilization of the nineteenth century, had become an almost fanatic advocate of communism. The fact that I had changed my mind after becoming familiar with the facts and circumstances, would compel the administration to treat me as a deceitful, unprincipled demagogue, if not as a scoundrel. There was very little doubt that I would be assigned to the most objectionable work, even if I was spared a term in an insane asylum. And how could I ask Edith Leete, blooming like a beautiful flower in a well protected garden, the house of her highly esteemed father, to join her lot to a man who would be regarded by most of the people either as a superficial babbler or as an unmasked hypocrite, deserving his fate to be degraded to class B of the third grade.

The fear of losing the love of Edith overshadowed for a while all other considerations, for I loved in Edith Leete Edith Bartlett! And the reflection that my resignation would cause the loss of Edith to me weighed upon my mind like a nightmare. Never in my life had I felt so distressed and miserable as on my way to Dr. Leete's house after my last conversation with Mr. Forest.

For a moment I harbored the idea of ending my misery by my own hand, but I resolved to be a man and face my fate. So I walked to Dr. Leete's house determined not to deceive my friends nor to shrink from my duty as a man of honor.

I found Dr. Leete, who generally appeared so gentle and composed, in a rather excited mood. He looked both careworn and threatening. Before I could address him he stepped in front of me and said:

"I have positive information that our mutual friend Mr. Fest, is plotting to incite a rebellion of the Radicals. Frequent secret meetings have taken place during the last few days, and I learn that Fest intends to start the rebellion here in Boston".

"What means will you employ to prevent it?" I asked. "Will you call out the citizens and arrest the conspirators? I am at your service", I added, very glad to demonstrate my readiness to serve my host at least against the Radicals whose abominable theories I hated—not to mention my dislike for their leader.

"I doubt very much whether it would be good policy to appeal to the people", replied the doctor. "Such a step would attach too much importance to the conspiracy. I wish I had placed that man Fest under medical care, when he left our house. He is the real danger of the hour. His followers do not amount to much, but under a leader like Fest, who combines a certain rude eloquence with reckless audacity and physical power, a rebellion may become a dangerous movement. To prevent this I have given orders to arrest the archconspirator and to put him in a safe place under medical treatment".

I could not indorse this step although it would, perhaps, prove successful. I suppressed my objections, however, and asked Dr. Leete if he could give a few minutes attention to my own affairs, for I considered it my duty not to keep secret my convictions any longer from Edith's father.

With his usual kindness Dr. Leete turned to me and requested me to defer the conversation until next morning if the delay would not be very disagreeable to me.

I consented.

We took our places at the table in the dining room.

Mrs. Leete had sent for a light supper to the common eating house, but none of us did justice to the meal. We all felt apprehensive.

Dr. Leete looked at his watch.

"By this time Fest ought to be in the care of the officers and physicians", he said. "I expect a report".

After a few uneasy minutes we heard a noise in the street, as if a great number of people were coming up to the house.

The housedoor was opened, and a brawling crowd entered the hall and pressed forward into the dining room. The mob was led by Fest, who, evidently, had just been through a hot fight. His woolen shirt was torn, and he swung a heavy butcher's axe stained with blood.

"Here I am again, Dr. Leete", he cried in his stentorian voice. "I gave you fair warning that I would not enter your house again as a friend. And since, you damned old hypocritical tyrant, you have given orders to imprison me in a mad-house, I have resolved that you shall die this evening. The people of Boston shall be relieved from your tyranny".

I seized a knife and stepping to the side of Dr. Leete, I stood ready to cover his body with my own.

But at this moment the mob's attention was distracted by the sudden appearance in the room of Forest, who jumped on the dining table and addressed the crowd without losing a second.

"I suppose you know who I am", he said. "I am an enemy of this man", and he pointed to Dr. Leete.

"Because I would not defend this miserable administration I was removed from my place as professor
of Shawmut College, and it was Dr. Leete who assigned me to the position of janitor".

"That's just like the miserable old tyrant", shouted
a dirty looking fellow.

"Therefore, I say: Down with an administration
that strangled free speech" continued Mr. Forest.
"Down with tyranny! But let us not butcher this
miserable old fellow. It is not worthy of young and
vigorous men like us to kill an unarmed old creature.
Let us place him in an insane asylum, where he intended to imprison our friend Fest".

"Yes, yes, put him in a madhouse", the mob yelled.

It was evident that Forest was trying to save Dr.
Leete's life. My eye wandered to Edith. She was
very pale but composed. She had put her left arm
around her father and she met my look with an expression of sympathy. Unfortunately, Fest noticed
that expression in Edith's eyes, and his jealousy broke
forth with increased force.

"You damned fools", he cried in a hoarse voice,
"don't you see that this man Forest is trying to save
the life of that tricky and dangerous old tyrant? But
I demand my share of the booty: the life of Leete
and his daughter"

"Do as you please, Bob"! the mob yelled.

"Leave this room, Forest", commanded Robert
Fest. "I have no grudge against you; but if you stand
in my way you will have to suffer the consequences".

"So long as I live you shall not commit murder in this house", Mr. Forest replied. "You ought to be ashamed, Fest, of a conduct so unworthy of a gentleman".

"Shut up, you fool", Fest screamed with rage. "That hypocritical scoundrel, Leete, has bulldozed the people long enough. He must die, and if you don't get out of our way, you will die with him".

A rage I had never felt before carried me away. "What has this old gentleman done to challenge your thirst for his blood, you mean, cruel coward?" I cried, and jumped at Fest, trying to put my knife into his heart. But a dozen fists disarmed me, while Fest commanded: "Put that old Bostonian in a bag and dump him in the harbor. Although not a gentleman in the eyes of the professor I am a man of my word, and I have promised that resurrected spectre, I would drown him like a puppy when ever again he crossed my path".

He lifted his axe and advanced towards Dr. Leete who remained silent, with his gray eyes fixed upon his brutal enemy.

Once more Forest tried to safe the life of the leader of the administration, but in vain. A dirty looking ruffian buried a knife in Forest's true and fearless breast and with the words: "We are even, Leete", he sank to the floor. Edith struggled with two men who had seized her arms and were trying to lead her away when Fest's axe descended on Dr. Leete's gray head. Without a murmur he fell to the ground, while Edith with a loud cry fainted. **Fest** seized her around her waist.

"She refused to be my wife" he said with a satanic grin, "now she will be mine without the ridiculous ceremony of marriage", and while stepping to the door with Edith's lifeless body clasped by his left arm he said: "Kill every friend of the administration, boys I will meet you at the city hall in an hour or so".

I made a tremendous, desperate effort to shake off the men who kept me back; I uttered a despairing cry and—awoke in my bed, May 31, 1887. At my bedside a physician, and my servant Sawyer had been busy for some time awakening me from my deep mesmeric slumber. They had labored very hard until they succeeded, but more than an hour passed before I had regained my ability of reasoning, and then I felt greatly relieved

With the swiftness of lightning all the details of my interesting but terrible dream passed through my mind. I weighed all the arguments of Dr. Leete and Mr. Forest carefully again, and felt delighted that I was living in the nineteenth century instead of in the communistic state that appeared to me now like a large penitentiary on the eve of a rebellion of the convicts.

"I would rather work harder at liberty than remain idle for a number of hours every day in a prison-like life", I said reflectively, "for work is not an evil. And I would rather work a few years longer and miss some commodities of life than submit to communistic slavery. Most of the luxuries for which we are strug-

gling appear most desirable so long as we do not possess them, and we do not care much for them when
they are ours".

I resolved to use hereafter my best ability for the
advancement of all desirable reforms for the benefit
of mankind, and to preach contentment, the only solid
basis of happiness. Felicity is so independent of
wealth, in fact glory and opulence are almost stum-
bling blocks in the way of happiness. Happiness depends largely on our acceptance of our lot. In
Victor Von Scheffel's famous poem "The Trumpeter
of Säckingen" young Werner when he parts from his
beloved Margaret, as he supposes forever, sings:

> To life belongs this most unpleasant feature:
> That not a rose without sharp thorns does grow.
> Though love eternal stirs our human nature
> Through pangs of parting we at last must go.

But Margaret is at last reunited to young Werner,
she becomes his wife, and it would have been much
more in consonance with the final result, if young
Werner, when departing from Margaret, had sung thus:

> To life belongs this very pleasant feature
> That next to thorns the blooming roses bend,
> And love eternal conquers human nature
> In joy uniting lovers in the end.

VAL. BLATZ BREWING CO.

MAIN OFFICE:

ERIE AND UNION STREETS.

HENRY LEEB,
Manager.

BOTTLING DEPARTMENT:

NO. 29 WEST OHIO STREET.

"EXCELSIOR,"
"PRIVATE STOCK."
"MUENCHENER,"

Delivered to Families.

Telephone No. 4382.

Chicago,   -   Illinois.

LADIES

If you are annoyed by the bones in your Corset breaking at the waist or hips, *try* the KABO CORSET, the boning material in it is warranted not to break or roll up with one year's wear

KIMBALL

PIANOS

INDORSED BY

ADELINA PATTI,
LILY LEHMAN,
SIG. TAMAGNO,
JULIUS PEROTTI,

GRAND ITALIAN OPERA CO.

METROPOLITAN OPERA CO.

BOSTON IDEAL OPERA CO.

and many other prominent artists.

FOR SALE BY

W. W. KIMBALL CO.

STATE & JACKSON STS.

www.ingramcontent.com/pod-product-compliance
Lightning Source LLC
Chambersburg PA
CBHW060245030726
47493CB00025B/2350